Unleashing the Shadows

A Paranormal Mystery

Matty Patterson Paranormal Series

Patti Frazee

ISBNs: 978-0-9984806-1-9 (print)
        978-0-9984806-2-6 (ebook)

Book and cover design: Patti Frazee
Cover image: IgorZh/Shutterstock

LynxGazer
Publishing

To Shannon
My paranormal partner
and a lifetime inspiration

Here's the thing. When I go to school, I see ghosts. Well, not really ghosts, but spirits. Yeah, that's right, dead people.

They're usually connected to my classmates. You know, grandpas and grandmas that died when my classmates were little.

What do they do? Well, nothing really. They kind of just stand off to the side and watch their grandkid. They're not always there, of course. I mean, I'm sure in the spirit world they have more important things to do than watch some teenager try to solve story problems in math class.

I don't know what brings them there at the times they show up. It's not like the kid is going through anything traumatic in math class. Maybe the kid thinks about their dead grandparent and the pull is so strong they just appear. I don't know.

Anyway, those aren't the spirits that intrigue me. The ones I'm drawn to are the ones who aren't connected to anyone. The ones who lurk in the shadows of the science lab or gym. They kind of look at me sideways and then disappear.

I don't get the sense they want anything from me. I get the sense…well, that they're watching me.

And that kind of creeps me out.

****

My bedroom is in the basement. I like that my mom and dad give me privacy. Not that I do anything particularly interesting.

I guess I'm kind of an unusual seventeen-year-old. I don't wear makeup and I don't like to talk about boys. I'm a tomboy. What does my mom expect when she nicknames me Matty? Matty is short for Mataya. I don't know where they got that name. Mom was a hippie or something.

Mom and Dad's bedroom is upstairs and my big sister Sasha is upstairs too. She's older than me. She graduated from high school last year and doesn't know if she wants to go to college or not, so she lives at home and goes out with her high school friends. They were all cheerleaders together. Well, what else can you do when your name is Sasha? Other than hide away in your room and write your secret poetry. Sometimes she goes to Omaha to read it at some coffeeshop in the Old Market.

I don't know, Sasha and I don't have much in common except our secret lives. Hers, poetry; mine, spirits that watch me from the corner of science lab.

Now, here I am, lying in bed, minding my own business, reading *Moby Dick* for English Lit, when it happens. My pencil rolls across my desk. At first, it makes me think of the calculus homework ahead of me, but then, a minute later, the pencil rolls back the same way.

Okay, there has to be a breeze or something, but my eyes are glued on that pencil and my butt is glued on the bed. Now the pencil doesn't move; it's resting in the exact spot it launched from. It's a new pencil, one I bought from a Spanish Club fundraiser for our end-of-school-year party. It's black with the word "*¡Escribe!*" on it in gold letters. The eraser is so new the pencil looks militant.

It's a dumb pencil, but I felt obligated to buy it, I mean, I had to buy something, being a member of Spanish Club, and it was either the pencil or a water bottle that said, "*¡Bebe!*" on it. The pencil seemed, well, less lame, so I went for the pencil. Plus, it's a #2 pencil, which is what I have to use for calculus.

It's stupid that the Spanish Club fundraising committee put such obvious commands on the pencil and water bottle, but then, no one asked for my opinion.

Just as I'm thinking all this, with my eyes still on the pencil, it rolls across the desk again, making a tiny click click click sound as each edge rolls.

As it rolls to the right again, I think maybe I should yell for Mom. But that didn't work out for me so well last time.

Click click click.

Maybe the pencil is rolling because my desk has always been a little off-kilter. Dad put it together when we moved here two years ago and he couldn't figure out how to level it. He's a lawyer, not a carpenter. At least that's what he said when he gave up putting the desk together.

Now the leaded end rises up and the pencil sits upright on the eraser end.

¡Mierda!

The air in the room feels heavy, like going to school on a foggy morning. The pencil stands there, slightly quivering, for like, five minutes. I swear to God. My eyes start to burn from staring at it so long.

Then the pencil drops and makes a little bounce. I finally breathe; I think I've been holding my breath this whole time. As I take in a big breath, I wait for the next trick of the Spanish Club pencil.

"Matty?" Mom calls from the top of the stairs.

"Yeah?" My voice croaks like it's real dry. I swallow, then say "yeah" again.

"Dinner's ready." The door shuts. I usually like that Mom and Dad give me privacy, but right now, I kinda wish Mom would have come down the stairs. I feel frozen, my eyes stuck on the pencil. But it's stopped moving and the air feels lighter now. I swallow again, hard, and move my eyes toward the stairs.

I can make it. I know I can. I jump off the bed and run up the stairs as fast as I can, taking them two at a time.

I try to act all normal when I get to the dinner table. It's unusual for both Mom and Dad to be at dinner. They're both lawyers and own a practice in Omaha. But they're between cases so here they are, together, taking an interest in my life.

"How was school today?" Mom asks. Sasha is spinning noodles onto her fork. Dad is waiting for an answer while he spins spins spins his noodles too.

"Good," I mumble, still trying to recover from what just happened in the basement. I never know what to say to Mom. It's not like I'm going to tell her about the pencil or the ghosts, and school is the same practically every day. Maybe I should give her access to my social media profile so she can see my updates.

"Anything special happen at school today?" She says it in a way that makes me think maybe something special did happen and I forgot about it.

I'm trying to decide if I should tell them what happened downstairs with the pencil just now, but I know what happened last time. "No," I shake my head, "I don't think so."

"Hmm." She's still looking at me.

I think hard. Did something special happen at school today?

"Mrs. Klein called me," she says.

Mrs. Klein is the gym teacher. Nothing happened to me in gym class. Except for that one ghost staring at me all the time.

"She wants you to try out for the basketball team next year. She said you're really good."

Oh yeah. I forgot about that. But I didn't know she was going to call my mom.

"Oh yeah. I forgot about that."

"Do you want to play basketball? It will be your senior year."

She always mentions my senior year when she thinks I need to show colleges more about what a valuable citizen I'll be on any campus.

"I don't know..." I actually like playing basketball, but the drills are torture, I swear.

"Well, you should think about it."

"Yeah. I will."

Social media update: Feeling inadequate and lazy due to my parents' disillusionment.

Sasha is still rolling pasta around on her fork. She looks bored. "What are you looking at weirdo?"

I guess I was staring too long or something. "Nothing." I can be snotty too.

"Girls..." Mom says it like she's going to give one of us a timeout even though we're both too old for that.

Sasha keeps twirling her pasta. "Are you going to eat it anytime soon?" I say to her. Still snotty.

"Matty!" Mom chastises me. "Come on, now, focus on your own plate."

Sasha flicks a chickpea from her salad at me. It flies past my head and lands somewhere on the floor behind me. What is she, ten? Mom and Dad didn't see it, so she gets away with it. I glare at her and shake my head while I sneer. I'm not going to play her game.

Then the chickpea flies back past my head and hits her square in the nose.

"Matty!" Mom yells loud this time. "Seriously! What's wrong with you?"

"Yeah, dork. What's wrong with you?" Sasha is rubbing the bridge of her nose as if it hurts as much as her pride.

"I didn't do anything!" I whine. But the minute it comes out of my mouth, I know I should take the blame for this chickpea-in-the-nose thing.

"Yeah, right." Sasha returns to her fork spinning.

"Matty…apologize to Sasha."

I have to pretend like I really did it. If Mom and Dad and Sasha knew what was going on right now—with the ghosts in classes and the pencil, and now the chickpea—God, I just can't put them through this again.

"I'm sorry Sasha." I choke out.

But what I really want to say is, "Who's here? And what do you want from me now?"

I sit in the family room with Mom and Dad and watch tv. Mom looks at me like I'm nuts. "You're going to sit here? With us?"

"Yeah. Why not?" I say as if it's no big deal. I usually watch tv in the basement in the comfort of my own room. Our old tv went to my room after we got the super high-def 65-inch Smart tv. My tv is not high-def, and is definitely not Smart, but it's mine so I really like it.

But tonight, I really don't want to be in the basement by myself. I also don't really want to watch D-list celebrities dancing with trained dancers, but hey, if that keeps me from a dancing Spanish Club pencil, then so be it.

Just as some "celebrity" I've never heard of is dancing the samba with some dancer I've never seen before, the room gets colder. Goosebumps rise on my arms. This is not a good sign.

Mom unconsciously pulls the throw from the back of the couch over her legs; Dad doesn't really seem to notice the temperature change.

I see a flash of light from the corner of my eye. I try to ignore it. That's what my psychologist told me to do.

"That was really good." Mom says to Dad.

"It was okay. Better than the tango they did last week."

"Well, the tango…" Mom goes on to talk about how difficult the tango is like she's presenting the case in court, but I'm not paying attention anymore because of the mist starting to form in the corner of the family room, just left of the tv.

It's getting so cold, I swear I can see Mom's breath. But Mom and Dad don't seem to notice anything—not the cold, not the mist—nothing.

I can't decide if I should keep my eyes on the tv and ignore the mist or keep my eyes on the mist. Before I can decide, the mist becomes a form. I see a hazy arm, then a gauzy white, then another arm, then a head.

The image is like looking into rippling water; it keeps quivering in and out of focus. But I can tell that the figure is a girl, like twelve years old, and she's looking at me with empty socket eyes.

I look at Mom and Dad, but they're both focused on the tv. They don't see her. At all. My lips begin to form the "m" of mom, but the girl holds up her palm, as if to tell me to stop. Then she slowly turns her hand around, tucks her thumb and last three fingers in so that just her index finger is raised.

I gulp.

She moves her index finger slowly, beckoning me to come to her.

No way. I kind of shake my head as I think it, my lips still pursed to form an "m."

But her index finger keeps moving like she's stuck and she can't stop it.

I move closer to Mom on the couch and again shake my head no.

"Matty, come on. You have that whole side of the couch for yourself!" Mom chastises me.

"Sorry." I say.

I look back to the corner and the girl is gone.

There's a part of me that wonders if it was all my imagination. But I know better. This girl is different than the others who have visited me. She, well, she…I gulp…she called out to me. Directly.

Mom laughs so loudly that I nearly jump off the cushion of the couch. I don't know what was so funny, but the audience laughs with her. Dad just kind of smiles.

My heart is still beating rapidly in my chest, but I just try to let things go. Again, advice from the psychologist. She said it was just stress from school and I needed to breathe deeply and count to ten whenever it happened again.

Breathe…1…2…3…4…

But I don't think this is stress.

…5…6…7…

I lay down with my head on the arm of the couch, my feet stretched out toward Mom. She puts her hand on my feet and I like it.

…8…9…10.

Mom takes the throw off her lap and puts it on my feet, then gives my calf a little squeeze.

If she only knew how much I needed that right now.

At school the next day, there's no way I'm saying anything to my friends about the Spanish Club pencil that did a dance on my desk. They wouldn't believe me anyway; at least that's what happened at my last school.

We're hanging out by the flagpole just like we do every morning. The end of the school year is just a few weeks away and Spring is in the air. We're all relieved to wear short sleeves again. I came to this school after the last incident happened. That was two years ago. I don't talk about that here because I don't want people to know me as the "poltergeist girl" or anything like that.

"Hey Matty," my friend Angie yells out to me, "there's that new boy." Her voice lilts at the end of the sentence and she gives me a nudge with her shoulder.

I thought he was nice the day I talked to him in Spanish class and told Angie. Geez, you say one thing and it turns into "Matty and Juan (his Spanish name) sittin' in a tree…"

"I don't like him that way. I just said he was nice."

"Yeah, nice and cuuuute!" Angie's voice rises on the last word. "Hola Juan!" She yells out and waves.

John waves back but he doesn't approach us.

"As if." I say to Angie. I play along because I haven't come out to my morning friends. I mean, Mom and Dad had to move us to a small town in Nebraska of all places. When they know that I like girls and I've liked them ever since I can remember. Anyway, Angie is not my best friend. My best friend is Kat. And she does know I'm gay. I just don't know if she knows that I have a massive crush on her.

Kat doesn't join us in the mornings because she likes to sit in a corner on the north side of the building listening to old punk rock music on some goofy cd player thing. Some people think it's weird that she's my best friend, but she's kind of like a ghost who's living, you know? I don't know; I just connect to her.

Emily says, "You guys want to go to the Juicy Burger after school and get some pop or something?"

Wait. Am I in a scene from *Grease*?

Angie puts her hand on her hip. "You just want to check out that cute guy that works behind the counter."

"I said 'or something...'" Emily giggles.

I get tired of the boy talk between these two, I have to admit. That's another thing I like about Kat, she doesn't spend all her time drooling over the lame boys here.

"Can't," I say.

"What have you got going on Miss Priss?" Angie says.

I try to make up something quick so I don't have to sit and watch them drool after school too. "I've got a report due on the Civil War tomorrow and I haven't really started it yet."

"Come on, you can come out for one glass of pop."

"Can't. My mom needs me to do some stuff around the house too." Lame, but it works; they just go on with their boy talk. Lewis this, Tony that, Mike so-and-so, cute boy in History...

Then over Emily's shoulder, I see her. It's the girl again. The one I saw last night at home. She seems more solid today; she's shimmering like water on a bright day. I can't really see through her like I could last night. And she's suspended in the air. I mean, she doesn't have any legs or feet. It's just her torso and head. She's looking at me, I swear it. She doesn't freak me out now as much as she did last night. I guess because she's so much further away. But I feel pulled toward her. Like I can't help but step closer.

I actually turn my back to Angie and Emily; one of them says my name. I manage to squeak out a "yeah, I'll be right back."

I step closer to the shimmering girl. She moves away from me at an equal pace, as if the energy between us was acting as a cushion. She's moving toward the library windows. I don't know how I notice, but there's no reflection of her in the glass.

I shift directions and walk parallel to her, keeping my eyes on her the whole time. Her head is turned; now I know she's watching me too.

She starts to fade, so I stop moving. She stops moving too.

Then she turns toward me and holds out both of her arms, like she wants me to hug her or something.

I don't move.

We stand there frozen, looking at each other. Her, with her arms stretched out, me with my mouth dry and palms sweaty. Then I hear a loud sound in my ears, like feedback on an amp at a rock concert. It screeches. I drop my messenger bag and throw my hands over my ears. My eyes stay glued on the girl, though, and as soon as the sound ends, she's gone. Just like that.

The first bell rings and it sounds so soft compared to the offensive sound that just filled my ears. Even while everyone moves around me to file into the school doors, I keep staring at that one spot where the girl was. Nothing happens.

Part of my brain is telling me "you don't want this." But the other part wants… I don't know…to know more. To find out who she is and why she's here. Or there. Or wherever she is.

I close my mouth and swallow down the dryness.

"Come on, Matty!" Angie grabs my arm and pulls me toward the doors. I blink my eyes and the burning tells me I haven't blinked in a while.

"Yeah," I take one last look toward the library windows and walk toward the building.

I don't want this I don't want this I don't want this runs through my head.

I see Kat in third-period English. She's got kind of a mini Mohawk going on today. It's very much *Girl with the Dragon Tatoo*-ish. Her eyes are as black as her hair today.

"I had on black lipstick, too, but that freaking Home Ec teacher made me take it off," she broods.

"That sucks." I don't know how to sympathize with her sometimes. I don't wear makeup myself. It takes too much time and I don't like how makeup feels on my face.

"Hey Kat," I lean into her desk and whisper, "I…" I debate about telling her about all what's been happening.

She looks at me expectantly, her brown eyes shining through the black makeup.

"Okay class, please turn to page 125," Mrs. Piorizini says. There's a rumor going around that her husband is a mob boss. I think it's bogus. A mob boss in small-town Nebraska? Get real. Dad says he's an insurance salesman.

Mrs. Piorzini is kind of a hard nose, so I tell Kat I'll talk to her after class.

And the class goes so slow. We're discussing *Moby Dick* and I think I'm going to die. Besides, every time Mrs. Piorzini says "Dick" the boys at the back of the class make goofy boy chuckle sounds. She ignores them, but still.

In the middle of class, a man appears behind Mrs. Piorzini. I mean a man-ghost. He's tall and he's wearing a black suit. Maybe that mob thing is true. He seems to be connected to her somehow, but he's looking at me. Staring is more like it.

The hairs on my arms stick straight up. I rub my arms, hoping no one has noticed. The man moves around Mrs. Piorzini but keeps his eyes on me. He's about her height and he has "the glow."

When I started seeing spirits five years ago, I named each way the ghosts appeared. Some spirits look gauzy, like how the girl looked last night. Some are transparent; they show up solid from head to toe but I can see right through them. Then there are the ones that glow; they are solid from head to toe too, but they burn bright, like there's too much light in them to be contained. They look kind of like a fluorescent lightbulb.

This spirit has the glow. But then he has this dark line around him. Like he's outlined. And he's staring at me. I'm sure of it. He puts his hand on Mrs. P's shoulder and she makes a move to adjust the sleeve of her blouse. That's usually how people react to a ghost's touch. It's that piece of itchy fabric, that slight skewed piece of clothing—they both end in some kind of adjustment by the wearer. If they only knew.

So Mrs. P adjusts the sleeve of her blouse and unwittingly moves away from the man. That leaves him with no one to hide behind and it makes it more obvious that he's staring at me.

I look away from him, to the floor, the ceiling, the boys in the back, anywhere just hoping that he looks away from me.

"Matilda?" Mrs. P interrupts my thoughts. "Are you okay?"

When I look back to the front of the classroom he's gone. "Oh, uh, yeah." I look back down at my book and Mrs. P continues talking. Then I feel a tug on my right shirt sleeve. I look to my side, but nothing's there. Until I feel his cold hand resting on my shoulder. It's the man. I know it's him. I can feel his presence and his hand is so cold it burns my shoulder. Ice cold. And the cold rises up to my cheek.

I flick my hand up to my right shoulder quickly and then try to look nonchalant, like I have an itch on my shoulder, my cheek, my neck.

Then he just goes away, but the coldness lingers until the bell rings.

"Matty?" Kat is shaking my left shoulder. Her hand is warm.

I stand up quickly.

"Man, you are really into *Moby Dick*, huh?"

"What?"

"Still thinking about it?"

"Huh? No," I feel like I'm drooling, I was so lost in the cold hand. I wipe my mouth, "No, I was just thinking about something."

Kat and I have lunch together every day. I'm the talkative one; Kat just usually watches people and listens to me blab on.

But today, we sit silently, moving food around on our plates. For a long time. At least until Kat says, "So what's up?"

I hesitate for a minute, then say, "I don't know. Nothing." I look down at my weird tuna noodle casserole. Why don't I bring my own lunch?

"No." Kat says, and then I realize she's staring at me.

"No?"

"Something's up. I know you." Her eyes are boring into me and I feel awkwardly uncomfortable.

I look away and shake my head.

We sit silent like that for a while.

Then Kat says, "You saw him, didn't you?"

Chills run down my spine. I look right at her. "Huh?"

She leans across the table as far as she can and whispers in a husky voice, "You saw him."

I don't know what to say. Is she talking about the glowing man for real? Or am I just hoping?

She leans back in her chair and twists a casserole noodle around her fork. "Yeah. You saw him."

"Are you talking about English Lit?" I don't want to give anything away. I don't think she does either.

"Mrs. P," she nods her head.

"Yeah?"

"Yeah."

We're just both sitting there nodding our heads like two stupid bobblehead dolls.

I finally say, "The man behind her?"

She twists her tongue around her teeth. "Yeah."

My heart is pounding in my chest and questions swirl around in my head. I want to know if she sees others too. But I'm afraid to ask.

"Is he yours?" she asks.

"What do you mean?"

"Does he belong to you? I mean, your family?"

"No." I gulp.

"Really?"

"Yeah." Now I'm wondering again if we're talking about the same thing.

"He was staring at you."

I nod my head.

"And he touched you."

My fork falls out of my hand, bounces off the table, and clatters onto the floor. "Yeah." Gulp again.

"I just thought he was connected to you."

"No."

"Huh." Kat looks confused. "I thought I read them better than that."

"Wait." I say and lean over the table toward her, "You see others?"

Kat looks concerned for a minute, like she just let out the biggest secret ever. She doesn't say a word.

"No..." I reach over and grab her arm. "I see them too."

Kat looks into my eyes. "Really?"

I nod emphatically and suddenly realize that my hand is resting on her arm. I remove it quickly.

"Holy..."

"Yeah," I say.

The bell rings.

"Shit..." Kat says.

"Can we talk later?" I ask. "Like, after school?"

"I gotta catch the bus." Kat lives on the other side of town.

"I can drive you. Please? We need to talk."

Kat doesn't even hesitate. "Yeah. We need to talk."

After school, Kat is waiting for me at my car. My heart beats a little faster every time I see her. Today she's wearing skinny black jeans and a vintage black B-52s shirt. She likes to shop at Goodwill. At least I think she likes it.

We met at school on my first day at Fremont High. It was in gym class and I was sitting on the mats off to the side. Kat sat down right next to me and said absolutely nothing. I think she wanted to get a reaction from me in some way: either because of the way she looked (which was not the cookie-cutter white-bread way of the other kids), or because she just plopped down without saying a word. Either way, I just started talking to her.

"Why don't we play football outside?" All of the girls were running around on the basketball court with the flags hanging from a belt around their waists.

"Coach is afraid of mosquitos," she said.

Okay, I thought. I didn't know if that was truth or a lie.

"How long you been here?"

"We just moved in over the summer," I answered. She stared at me through her long bangs. "July 1st."

"Thought I saw you at the fireworks on the 4th."

"Oh yeah?" *Huh,* I thought. *She noticed me.*

"They're lame," she said. "The fireworks. Where you from?"

"Oh, ah, Denver." And before she had a chance to ask anything else, I added, "Mom and Dad wanted to be close to Omaha. They're both lawyers and wanted to start a practice there. Corporate law. Mom worked at some big law firm in Denver but it took her more than an hour to get to work and she was tired of working in such a big firm. She always wanted to start her own firm but Denver is overrun with lawyers and she thought she could make a go of it here, you know, because of Warren Buffet and all, and the opportunities with big business in a smaller city…" And by the time I got to Warren Buffet I realized I was talking too much, but I had to finish my sentence.

God, I'm boring.

"Well, if you ever want to hang out…"

By lunchtime, we had exchanged numbers. I guess being from Denver and being a lesbian made me different than everyone else. I thought that maybe she liked me, I mean, as more than a friend, but then she started talking about some skateboarder dude in Omaha that she liked. Unlucky me, by then I had developed a little crush on her.

Now I just want to brush away the long bangs that hang off her forehead so I can see her smoky eyes better. Instead, I jiggle my keys as I approach the car. "Hey," I say.

"Hey," she says back. Then we silently get into the car. The temperature is just right in the car—not too hot, not too cool.

"So?" I say as I put the keys in the ignition. "Where should we go?"

"Let's go out to the lakes. I know a good place where no one can hear us talking."

"Okay." I turn the engine on and head out toward the lakes. We talk about stupid stuff on the way out there. Classes, homework, the girls we know at school. We don't say anything about the ghosts we see. Well, I guess I don't know how many she sees anyway.

I turn off onto a dirt road. Kat directs me to a picnic table surrounded by trees. I ignore the creepy factor of this remote location.

We walk down to the lake and stand at the edge of the water. Kat picks up a few small rocks and skims them on the surface of the lake. Of course, she gets like four bounces on the first try. She doesn't say anything for a while, so I pick up some small pebbles and start to do the same, only my first few plop into the lake without a bounce.

"When did it start for you?" Kat finally asks. "The ghosts." She doesn't even hesitate.

I lie because I don't want her to think I'm a total weirdo. "Twelve."

"I was eight."

"Wow. Were you scared?"

"No. They mostly just walked through my room in this old house we lived in." The rock she throws skips six times.

"Do you remember any of them?"

"Yeah. The first one was this grandpa guy. His name was Arnie. He was nice. He'd just kind of say hi on the way through."

"He talked to you? And told you his name?" Goosebumps rise on my arms. I can't imagine any ghosts being nice to me like that.

"Oh yeah. Then Chrissy showed up. She only had one arm, but we used to play Barbie's together."

OMG. Kat used to play with Barbies?

"Yeah, I know," she says as if reading my mind, "hard to imagine."

"Yeah...exactly." I laugh. Kat smiles.

"Mine were never that nice," I say. The next rock I throw lands with a big plop. No skips.

"Really?" Kat looks at me.

"Yeah. They've always been..." I look around as if they're watching me right now, so I whisper, "well...kinda mean."

"Mean? Like how?"

Do I dare tell her? I mean, this is why we moved the last time; this is what got me into therapy. And what if I open this box and all the ghosts come back, like the ones in *Ghostbusters*?

"Matty?" Kat's hand rests on my forearm as she waits for my answer.

"I…I don't know if I should say it." I'm nervous and I don't know if it's because of the ghost talk or because of her hand sitting there, on my arm.

As if she senses my confusion, she lets go of my forearm. "Was it that bad?"

She doesn't say it in a condescending way, or a hurtful way, but I feel kind of like she doesn't believe me.

I swallow hard. "It was pretty bad."

"Shit."

That's all she says.

We sit there silently for a few minutes and then, I don't know what happens to me, but I spill my guts. "It started when I was twelve…" It's like the space and the silence she gave me let me trust her or something. "At first it was just a shadow that crawled around my bed at night. It scared me, but my mom told me it was just the tree outside swaying in the wind and casting shadows all over my room.

"I believed her until the bed started to shake. At first it was just like a bump, but then it was like I was a kernel of popcorn in the microwave."

Kat sits down on the shore and tugs on my sleeve to sit down next to her, "How long did the shaking last?"

"Like a minute, long enough to be scary but short enough to make me wonder if it really happened."

Kat pulls her knees to her chest. She's looking out at the water, but I know she's still listening.

I cross my legs and lean back on my hands. "And then this guy showed up. I mean, he was a guy, but he wasn't really a guy… you know?"

Kat shakes her head no.

"He was like a…a shadow grown-up. Dark and scary. He was tall and…and scary…like I could see him, but he didn't really have a face. But I knew he was staring at me. I could feel his eyes watching me. He was kind of like a creepy guy that will stare at kids at the park but not do anything…he would just watch me from the distance." I stop and brush sand off my pantleg. "And the room would get real cold, you know? Like a refrigerator." Kat doesn't say anything, she just kind of nods her head but I can tell her ghosts never froze her out. "But he wasn't as scary as the next thing…"

"Crap. There's more?"

A lot more I wanted to say but wasn't sure how far I was going to go here.

"Yeah. Then one night, I woke up and I was floating." I kind of look at Kat out of the corner of my eye to gauge her reaction. She's still with me, listening intently. I swallow. "Like, two feet off the bed and then this loud whoosh started moving around me and then…well, I started spinning in the air."

"Spinning?"

"Not real fast, but enough to make me dizzy. And that's when I screamed—screamed my head off for my mom. I was just yelling and yelling and I couldn't even really hear myself because it sounded like a train in my ears, like a tornado or something. And then, all the sudden, Mom was standing over me, shaking my shoulders like I had just been dreaming or something. She was yelling 'Matty, Matty…wake up!' That's when I realized that the room was still spinning but I wasn't. And my feet were on top of the pillows and my head was on top of the covers and Mom pulled me toward her and told me it was all just a bad dream. And I let her believe it because it even made me wonder. But I know it happened."

"Wow." Kat sounds slightly disappointed, like maybe I'm not in the ghost club with her or something. "Is that all?"

I kind of feel mad about how she says that and I say snotty-like, "No, then the next night I felt this burning pain on my back, like someone put a hot branding iron on me. It hurt so bad that I went in my mom and dad's room and woke up my mom. She looked at my back and there were three long scratches on my skin, right below my left ribcage. Mom took me to the bathroom and started putting ointment on it and that's when I told her about all the other stuff…the shadow man and the spinning. She already knew about the shaking bed.

"A few days later Mom asked me to go see this doctor. It ended up that I was seeing a psychologist. Turns out that Mom thought I put those scratches on my back myself 'cuz the doctor asked me if I had ever cut myself before."

"They thought you were a cutter?"

"Yeah." I feel my chin quiver remembering all of this, but I'm not gonna cry. I swear I won't.

"Wow."

Now I feel like I've got her attention, so I go on. "But then things started happening to them too. All of our windows would blow open in the middle of the night when there was no wind outside, and all the chairs around the dining room table would be turned over and sitting on top of the table like they do in restaurants, and stuff would be knocked off shelves. And then Dad woke up one night with the scratches on his arm and face."

Kat is sitting there listening intently. She doesn't say a word.

"That was the night that I saw the man in the shadow again, only this time he was looking right down on me in bed. I felt this cold air on my face like his ice-cold breath was bearing down on me. He just stared at me and I tried to get up, but I couldn't move—not my arms, not my legs—nothing, it was like I was stuck to the bed. I started screaming but the windows busted open at the same time and made this huge noise in the house, so Mom and Dad were running around the house trying to shut the windows that kept popping open and they didn't hear me.

"That went on for like ten minutes when Mom finally came in my bedroom. She tried to pull me out of the bed but she couldn't; the man was still holding me down. She yelled 'let go right now' and suddenly I was free. Then everything just stopped in the house.

"Mom and Dad huddled with me on the bed and Mom and I cried for a while. A couple days later they told me we were moving and we moved here. Everything stopped after that."

"Until now," Kat says nodding.

"Yeah, until now."

"Do your parents know?"

"No."

"Are you going to tell them?"

"I don't know. The ghosts aren't as bad this time. You know? Like, they just watch me in classes mostly, but I don't feel scared by them. They're not like the shadow man. They seem more like they're reaching out or something."

"When did they start showing up?"

"I don't know, about a month ago."

"Right after Spring break?"

I think for a minute. "Yeah, I'd say that's about right."

"Yeah. That's when I started seeing them again too."

Then she stands up and wipes the sand off her butt. She extends her hand to help me up. I look out at the water and say, "I'm not gonna be scared this time. I'm not scared this time."

It helps to think that someone else knows what's going on.

My fearlessness lasted only until the sun went down. I ended up watching tv with Mom and Dad again, at least until I fell asleep. We'd been watching a cooking show and now I'm dreaming about chopping onions in a teen challenge.

"Matty," Mom whispers. She shakes me awake. "It's time to go to bed."

I want to ask her if I can just stay here on the couch. Or if I can sleep in the bed with her and Dad can sleep on the couch. But I'm not a baby.

It'll be okay.

"Matty…"

"Okay Mom."

I take the throw with me as I drag myself off the couch. Like it's a security blanket or something. I drag my feet across the floor as I head toward the basement door.

Mom gives me a kiss and I want to beg her to let me stay with her tonight.

I turn the handle to the basement door. "'Night Mom."

"'Night honey."

I turn on the light at the top of the steps and wait. For what, I don't know. For something to move or something, I guess.

I really wish we had a dog. I would send the dog down first

to make sure it was all okay. But what if the dog didn't go down the stairs?

Okay, this is ridiculous. Nothing's going to happen. It's just my room.

I step down one, two, three stairs. The fourth stair creaks. I stop. Nothing.

I run down the stairs, hit the light switch, and jump on my bed. I keep my eyes closed as I pull the covers and dive underneath them. I pull the covers tight under my chin.

1...2...3...4...

Shoot! I'm still wearing my pants. I pull them off as I count.

5...6...

That's all the further I get.

That's when everything starts to happen.

I park in the back lot of the school today to avoid seeing Angie and Emily. I can't let them see me like this, the same way I couldn't let Mom see me this morning. I just grabbed my backpack and ran out the door yelling a good-bye behind me.

I do not want to see a psychologist again, that's for sure.

I keep my head down as I walk toward the tennis courts. I don't want anyone to see the long red scratch on my neck.

Kat is exactly where I thought she'd be. Leaning back on the tennis court fence, headphones over her ears. I think her mom must've given her that old portable cd player with old foam headphones. She listens to it like her life depends on it.

"Kat!" I whisper kind of loud, but of course she can't hear me.

I tap her shoe with my shoe.

She looks up and the sun must be in her eyes because she's squinting up at me. She's moving her head around to the music that fills her ears.

I kneel down in front of her and she pulls the headphones off. I can hear the music screeching out around her neck.

"Hey," she says.

"Kat..."

"Crap. What happened to you? Stay up too late doing your homework?"

I pull down the army-print buff around my neck that is way too hot to wear in late April.

"What's that?!?" Kat sits up straight. She fumbles with the clunky round cd player to turn off the music.

"Something happened last night."

Kat runs her finger over the bright red scratch. It runs from under my right ear, across my throat, down to my left collarbone.

"It feels hot. What the frick happened to you?!?"

I sit down next to her and lean back against the fence. I gulp hard. "I had a bad night last night, Kat."

"Was it the ghost from Mrs. P's class?"

"It was him… and others."

"Others? Like, how many?"

"I don't know. Three or four maybe."

"Four!" Kat sits up and turns toward me. She puts her hands on my knees. My heart beats a little faster. "Tell me!"

I hesitate, but then let it all out. "I knew it wasn't going to be a good night. I could feel it. I even watched tv with my parents again last night to avoid my room. It's in the basement and lately, I don't know, it just kind of freaks me out."

Kat nods at this.

"So, I was lying in bed, trying to get to sleep, except the air was so thick and heavy, and cold at the same time, you know?"

Kat nods again, and I somehow believe that she knows what I mean.

"That's when this shadow moved across my wall. It was a man for sure, and he was tall, like all the way up to the ceiling tall. Then the shadow just kind of disappeared into the wall. And then this tapping sound started, like from inside the wall." I tap a slow, rhythmic beat on my phone with my index finger. "Like that. Kind of quiet but persistent.

"Then, I saw the guy from Mrs. P's class. He was just standing in the corner watching me, then poof! He was gone. That's when I heard footsteps on the stairs. Something was coming down the stairs so slowly, I thought I'd scream or cry or something. But I just swallowed hard and pulled the sheets up to my nose. And

I saw the legs coming down the stairs. They were kind of gauzy and glowing. I should have seen a whole body by the time I saw the legs, but there was no body. Only these legs coming down the stairs, one at a time, very very slowly." Even though living this all over again scared me, I was kind of getting into it because of the attention I was getting from Kat. I was drawing out my words ve… ry… slooooooow…ly.

"As the legs got closer, a body started to appear above them. It was this old lady with silver hair. She was all hunched over and had these long, thin fingers. She walked toward my bed and stopped right at the foot of it. Then she reached down with her long fingers and grabbed my feet, but not in a mean way, you know? Kind of like," I placed my hands on Kat's feet and squeezed in the same way the weird ghost lady did to me. "It was in a loving way, but her fingers were ice cold and I could feel that all the way through my blanket. Ice-cold fingers." I let go of Kat's feet and shudder, feeling more freaked out about it now than I did when it was happening.

"Yeah?" Kat shakes me out of my wandering mind. "Then what? Did you talk to her? Did you ask her what she wanted?"

I swallow hard. "Talk to her? No way. She scared me."

"Yeah, but, didn't you want to know what she wanted from you?"

I shake my head quickly, "Not really."

"Oh, I would've talked to her. I would've asked her questions."

That didn't even occur to me. I continue, "Well, then the tapping started again, behind the wall, or in the wall, or whatever. The lady, she looked away from me and toward the tapping. Then she slowly moved to the wall and walked into it.

"That's when the shadow crossed in front of me again and disappeared up the stairs. And, I don't know, I guess I was watching the shadow and didn't notice what else was going on in the room, but then I felt this hand on my shoulder. It was the girl I've seen before…"

"What girl?"

"She has these black-socket eyes and no legs. She's a floater. I first saw her in our living room, but the next day she showed up outside school, by the library. Last night, she was floating next to my bed. She didn't touch me for long, just a few seconds, and then she made a moaning kind of sound, like she wanted to talk but couldn't. She gave me the heebie jeebies. Then she quickly looked…as much as an eyeless being can… back to the stairs and then she was gone.

"But that's when the shadow appeared again and this loud screeching filled the room, or my ears, I don't know…it didn't seem to wake Mom and Dad or Sasha."

"Screeching? What kind of screeching? Like an animal?"

"No, not an animal, like a microphone that has feedback or a guitar amp or something. Mechanical, I guess, but real loud." I try to make the sound with my own voice and start to cough as I inhale the noise. "I've heard it before and I hate it."

"Where did you hear it before?"

"I don't know…just sometimes. I just close my eyes and cover my ears to try to block it out, but it's like it's inside my ears or something. Anyway, that's when I felt this burning on my neck. And then everything just stopped."

"Stopped?"

"Yeah, the room became dead silent and still. Nothing moved. No shadows, no nothing. But my neck burned all night and when I looked in the mirror this morning—well, this is what I saw." I pull down my buff and show Kat the long red scratch again.

"Crap."

I shake my head. "Do you have some kind of makeup to cover it up?"

"Yeah, sure." Kat digs in her backpack and pulls out some skin-colored makeup. I don't know anything about makeup, but I'm sure glad she does. She starts dabbing it on my neck as I hold down the buff.

"Matty…" She dabs dabs dabs makeup as she talks. "I know someone who might be able to help."

Oh, here we go. "I already saw a shrink once for this, Kat."

"A shrink?" Kat looks offended. "No, it's my cousin in Omaha. He's a ghost hunter."

"Like those guys on TV?"

She nods, "He belongs to the OPS."

"The OPS?"

"Omaha Paranormal Society," she says matter-of-factly, like I should've known what she meant.

"Oh."

She puts the cap back on the foundation and rubs her finger to get the excess makeup off. "I think he can help."

"Yeah, well, can he do it without my parents knowing? They're not too keen on me and ghosts. They think I'm crazy or something."

"I think so. I can ask him. But maybe he can at least tell us what's going on." She takes out her phone. "Should I call him?"

"Now?"

"Well, not now, he works, you know, like, a real job. But after school maybe?"

"Yeah," I don't say it with a lot of conviction, but then it starts to sink in. "Yeah, okay. I mean, I can't live like this."

"Nah. You look kind of zombielike today."

I'm really glad I have Kat on my side. Glad that I finally have someone I can talk to.

After school, Kat and I meet in the parking lot by my car.

"See anything today?" Kat asks.

"Just the usual…grandmas and grandpas standing next to their grandkids. You?"

"Yeah. Just one old lady standing next to Senorita Schroeder."

Our Spanish teacher. She spent three years in Guatemala in the Peace Corps. But when Kat says "old lady," it makes me think of something.

"You know, I've never seen my grandparents."

Kat leans back on my car. "And?"

"Well, I mean, I've seen my dad's mom, she's still alive, but the rest of my grandparents died before I was born or when I was young."

"Geez. What kind of genes are in your family?"

"I know, right?" I count them off on my fingers, "Heart attack, heart attack, cancer."

"Man…"

"But listen, maybe I have seen my grandparents. How do I know if one of the ghosts I've seen isn't them?"

"But you've seen pictures, right?" Kat digs a lighter from her backpack. She doesn't smoke, she just likes fire, I guess. She starts to flick it on and off, mindlessly watching the flame dance.

"Yeah, but it's been forever. Maybe we should go to my house and look through some old pictures. Like, maybe the guy that touched me in Mrs. P's class was my grandpa or something."

"Good idea." Kat holds a flame up in front of her face, then releases the button on the lighter. The flame instantly disappears. She looks at her watch. "I don't think my cousin is off work until five or something. He's got a normal job in some office."

"So, we go to my house, look through some old pictures, and then call your cousin."

"Let's go!" Kat sounds like she's in some action tv show. I believe if I had a convertible, she would have jumped in over the door.

For a moment, I have the sinking feeling that my mom won't like the looks of Kat, with her mini Mohawk and all. But Mom won't be home from work until 5:30 or 6:00, so maybe she won't even see Kat.

When we get to my house, I try to think of the last place I saw the photo album that has all the old photos in it, from before Sasha and I were born. There are tons of albums filled with photos of me and Sasha, but I don't care about those. Kat waits in the living room while I dig through a stack of albums in the closet in the office. I have a moment of hoping that she's not looking at our goofy framed family photos, but then I realize I'm about to show her our unframed goofy family photos.

I finally find the album, buried behind a stack of papers. If I didn't know how messy my dad's closets were, I'd think my parents were hiding this.

When I get back to the living room, Kat is looking at a framed photo of my family. "Cute," she says matter-of-factly, and I kind of wonder if she's teasing me.

"Mom's Valentine's gift last year. Dad thought it would be fun if we all went and got a professional picture taken. Lame."

"No, that's kinda cool, that your dad would do that."

Cool is not how I would describe that photo. And it's definitely not how I would describe my dad. He's a lawyer like mom. Corporate law. And he likes to tell goofy dad jokes.

"Here it is," I raise the album next to my head. It's surprisingly heavy, so I drop it into my other hand like a sack of flour.

I sit down next to Kat on the sofa and wipe dust off the green cover of the book. "I think my mom inherited this from my grandma after she died."

"Like it was in your grandma's will or something?"

"No, she just took it from her house, I think. Her sister didn't want it, I guess."

Kat looks at me like she's waiting for me to tell her some juicy story of a family fight or something, but there's no story to tell. I don't even really know how Mom ended up with this album.

I open the front page. There are a lot of black-and-white images with white borders around them, and nearly every image has writing in blue ink along the bottom. "June's first birthday," "June in pool," "June with doll."

"Who's June?" Kat asks.

"That's my mom."

Kat looks from the photos to my face a couple of times. "Oh yeah, I can see it," she says like she sees a resemblance.

"Right," I say sarcastically.

Kat smiles and looks back at the album. I turn the page and there are more photos of my mom doing various activities. I turn another page and another.

My eyes land on one particular picture. I drop my finger on it.

"What?" Kat says.

I wonder if my eyes are as wide open as they feel.

"Her." I say, "Oh. My. God."

Kat and I are still staring at the photo album when Mom gets home from work. She greets me as she stands in the entryway taking off her shoes. "Who's your friend?"

I take my eyes away from the photo album. We've found four other photos of the woman, all of them with no writing anywhere on the photo to indicate who she is. "Ah, this is Kat. She's my friend from school."

"Kat?" Mom seems to be thinking through the list of names I've mentioned at the dinner table. "Oh, from your gym class." She's good. I didn't think she paid that much attention to me when I talked about my friends at school.

"Yeah. Mom? Who's this woman in these photos?"

Mom stands behind the sofa and peers over my shoulder at the photo album. "That?" She points to the elderly woman with white hair. In this picture, she's sitting behind a cake.

"Yeah."

"That is my great-grandma, your great-great-grandma."

Kat and I exchange a look. "Like, when did she die?"

"Oh gosh. Before you were born. I was a about seven or eight years old when she died."

"Was she kind of hunched over?"

"Yeah, she was. She must've had osteoporosis or something. She moved pretty slow. Why do you want to know?"

"Oh," that question takes me by surprise. I hope I don't look as flustered on the outside as I feel on the inside. After a minute of staring at her quizzical look, I come up with an answer. "We're supposed to do a paper in our history class on someone in our family. I found her picture and thought she looked interesting." *Pretty good, Matty, pretty good.*

"Good choice! She was an interesting character."

"Really?"

"Oh yes, you know she grew up in a time when women were only housewives; they didn't work, they followed their husbands, they obeyed their fathers."

Kat and I both crinkle our noses.

"Oh yeah. She was born in 1890. Women weren't even allowed to vote back then when she was growing up. That's just how it was." Mom squeezes in between me and Kat, like she's going to impart some great lesson about history or something. *Keep it short, Mom,* I think. "But she was feisty. She was different. She didn't want to be held back by men." Mom sticks her index finger up in the air as if to punctuate this: "*Any men.*"

She pauses like we need time to absorb all this. We don't.

"She went to college. That was unusual for a woman in her time. And she didn't even become a nurse or a teacher. She went into the sciences. Astronomy or something, I don't really remember, but she could point out every star in the sky and tell you what it was.

"Whatever career she wanted to have was sidetracked by getting married and having kids. Women didn't have both a career and family back then. So, she became a housewife in the end." Mom sighed as if some great injustice to women had to leave her body.

"But you remember her from when you were little?" I ask.

"Oh yeah…like I said, she could point out every star in the sky. That's what she'd do with us great-grandkids. I remember her taking us out to the back porch of her house at night and pointing out Orion, the Big Dipper, Jupiter; any star or planet that might have been making an appearance. And when something special happened, like the Northern Lights or something, we would go to great-grandma's house like it was Thanksgiving. We would all stay overnight and she would wake us kids up when the Lights would come out. She said it was important for us to be connected to the sky."

I look down at the picture in the photo album. Her eyes look clear and bright even though she looked a hundred in the photo. "What was her name?"

"Myrtle."

"Myrtle? Really?"

"It was just a name women had back then."

"Myrtle," I say, as if letting the name settle in my head.

"Well," Mom grabs my knee and hoists herself off the couch, "I'll leave you girls to the research. Does your Mom know where you are, Kat?"

I roll my eyes, but Kat shows more respect and politely answers, "She works second shift so she doesn't get home 'til ten." My heart falls. Mom probably thinks Kat is a bad influence or something and we'll have some big fight about me not hanging out with her. Great.

"Oh. And your dad?"

"Divorced. He lives in Seattle. I see him every now and then."

"Oh," Mom looks disappointed. "Do you want to stay for dinner?"

"Nah, that's okay. My mom leaves dinner made for me already."

"Oh." With that Mom leaves the room. She seems kind of stunned.

I'm not sure where this will go. But I have more important things to discuss right now. "Kat!" I poke my finger at the photo album. "*This* is the lady! My great-great-grandma!"

"The lady...?"

"With the ice-cold fingers and the body-less legs! The one who showed up in my room when everything went crazy. She held onto my feet."

Kat studies the photo under my index finger. "What do you think she wanted?"

"I don't know, but maybe she'll show up again. And maybe I won't be so freaked out and I'll try to talk to her."

Kat leans back on the couch. "Do you think she'll show again?"

"I don't know." I hope she does. "Can we call your cousin in Omaha yet?"

Kat pulls out her cell phone. "Well, it's 5:45; let's try." She starts tapping her phone with her thumbs.

"Wait!" I yell-whisper. "Let's go down in the basement." I don't want Mom to overhear us talking about ghosts with Kat's cousin.

We sit on the couch downstairs and Kat sits right next to me. I mean, our arms and legs are touching. Is she trying to flirt with me?

But her thoughts are totally on the phone in her hand. She has it on speakerphone when it starts ringing.

Two rings, three rings. My heart is pounding. I don't even know why.

Four rings, five… Crap! We'll have to leave a message; I just know it. What will Kat say? *Hey, my friend is having some crazy experiences and needs a ghostbuster.*

"Hello, this is Jason." a young voice comes over the line, but his manner is old and…businesslike.

"Hey Jace, it's Kat," Kat sounds so cool. I wish I could be like her.

"Katrina," Jason relaxes his tone.

"Katrina?" I ask.

"Shut up," Kat says. "It's a family name. My great-grandma came from Russia."

I snicker anyway.

"How's it going?" Jason asks.

"Good. I have my friend Matty here. She's listening on speaker."

"Hi Matty," Jason sounds friendly, easy-going like Katrina. Lol.

"Hi," my voice comes out all timid and high-pitched and stupid.

"She's been having some stuff happen." Wow. *Way to cut to*

the chase, Kat. "Some of it is pretty tame and usual, like spirits showing up in class and stuff. But some of it is more violent…like scratches and levitation and stuff."

"No shit?"

Wow. Very different than Jason businessman.

"Are you a channeler, Matty?"

I look at Kat stupidly. "I don't know," I shrug my shoulders.

"Do you communicate with the spirits?" Kat says as Jason listens to us.

"Oh. No way."

Kat clucks her tongue like I just said the wrong answer.

"Um. Okay," I say. "Do they communicate with you, Katrina?"

"You mean, like actually *talk*?"

"Well, yeah."

"No."

I laugh and shoulder bump Kat. She just smiles back.

"Matty, how many spirits do you see?" Jason's voice asks.

"Sometimes just one; other times, like, ten or more."

There's silence for a moment, then Jason says, "Can you guys get to Omaha? Can we meet in person?"

Kat looks at me since I'm the one with the car.

"Yeah. Well, I can get to the Village Pointe Mall for sure."

"Hold on, let me check my calendar." I assume his calendar is on his phone based on the shuffling I hear on the other end. "What are you guys up to this weekend? Can you meet at the coffeeshop at Village Pointe?"

Kat nods her head.

Wait. Let me check my calendar. Yep. Looks like I have absolutely nothing going on. "Yeah. Saturday afternoon?"

I give Jason my phone number and wonder how I'll tell Mom I need to go to Omaha on Saturday.

It's a beautiful day in the stark Nebraska countryside. The farmers are starting to plow their fields to get ready for planting. There's a warm breeze from the south and not a cloud in the sky. Kat and I have the windows rolled down; it's a good thing we both have short haircuts, still Kat's long bangs fly around her eyes in the wind. Every now and then she runs her fingers through her long bangs and flips them back.

I don't know what kind of music to play, so we ride in silence. I don't want to be uncool with her and I don't really know any 80s punk music.

When we're not talking about ghosts, we don't seem to have anything to talk about, so it's a long ride. Kat picks at chipped black nail polish on her left index finger.

"Cool nail polish." *Stupid!*

"Thanks." She's unimpressed.

I sigh.

I told my mom that Kat needed to get some money from her cousin so that she and her mom could get groceries. I know I played on my mom's assumptions about Kat's "situation," as Mom now calls it, but what else was I supposed to do? I couldn't let her know these things were happening again.

I look over at Kat and feel bad that I used her. I don't even know if she and her mom are struggling. I know Kat's clothes come from Goodwill, but maybe that's a choice.

Kat's cute. She has an innocent face despite the black eyeliner and dark eye shadow. It's almost like that's what she's hiding. Innocence.

"So how long has your cousin been a ghost hunter?" I ask.

She looks straight ahead, as if she has to watch the road as much as I do. "Since he was eighteen. It was his mom's eighteenth birthday gift to him; to let him become a ghost hunter. He had begged her since he was like twelve or something."

"How did he know where to go?"

"He looked it up on the Internet and found OPS." She pulls her bangs to the side and holds them there for a minute. "They said they would try him out for a few months, but they realized how serious he was about it and signed him up for good. He loves it."

"Does he have a lot of stories about it? I mean, I'd think he would."

"He doesn't talk about it all that much cuz his mom doesn't really like it. I think it freaks her out." She lets go of her bangs and they fly around her eyes again. "And I don't really see him other than at family gatherings." She bites the end of her black fingernail.

Kat turns on the radio in my car and I feel my face turn beet red when the Top 40 station comes on. She must think I'm the biggest nerd. But she doesn't say anything. She just looks out the front window and watches the empty fields pass by.

A good-looking dark-haired guy waves at us when we walk into the coffeeshop. He's wearing a t-shirt and jeans; not the office attire I expected. "Hey Katrina!" he stands and gives Kat a kiss on the cheek. I try not to snicker at "Katrina" again. He extends his hand to me and says, "Jason."

"Matty," I say as I awkwardly shake his hand. He has deep blue eyes and dimples.

He motions for us to sit down at the small table with him. "You two want anything to drink? A mocha mocha latte coca mocha?" His eyes actually twinkle when he tells a joke. No lying!

Kat and I place some orders and Jason graciously pays. We argue that we should be buying his drink but he insists, saying we drove the half hour to meet him here.

Kat and Jason stand and wait for the drinks while I hold a table for us. Then, this woman sits down next to me and introduces herself as LuAnn. "I'm here with Jason."

"Oh. Uh, I'm Matty." I put my hand out for her to shake it, but she just looks into my eyes.

LuAnn is old: like, wrinkly old. She has white, shoulder-length hair and deep-set eyes surrounded by soft wrinkles. Her face looks freshly powdered with a touch of blush. She is thin and seems tall because she sits so upright and straight, but I bet she's only 5'3" or something. I guess she must be in good shape.

"I can help you," she says.

A chill runs down my spine.

Jason sets a latte in front of me and then turns back to the counter to wait for his drink.

I turn my attention back to LuAnn.

"What do you mean?" I ask her.

"You're psychic." She tugs on the bottom of her flowy blouse. It's made of silk or something.

"Huh?"

"You see them. You and Kat. But you're more in tune than she is."

Jason and Kat sit down at the table. Thank god. I've had enough of this LuAnn lady already.

Jason blows steam off the top of his coffee. "So Matty, you've been having some activity?"

I take a sip of my latte and nearly burn my tongue off, but I try to play it cool. "Yeah, uh, like, I see dead people all the time, but things have been getting kind of out of control."

"That's what Kat said."

I pull up my short sleeve up to show him some bright red scratches on my shoulder. "I got these last night."

He runs his fingertip across them, then says, "Did you feel it when it happened?"

"It woke me up."

"So you were sleeping?"

"Yeah," I wonder if he thinks I did it myself, while I was sleeping. "I felt this burning on my arm and it woke me up…and then this…" I rub my shoulder where the scratches are.

"Huh." He leans back in his chair in contemplation.

LuAnn just keeps staring at me, like she's sizing me up or something. #Creepy.

Kat is talking, and LuAnn's mouth is not moving, but her voice is in my head. "I see you, Matty Patterson. We have a lot of work to do."

Literally, her lips did. Not. Move. Not one bit.

LuAnn keeps her eyes on me and I squirm in my chair.

"Matty?" Jason says.

I break eye contact with LuAnn. "Huh?" It's like I was in a trance.

"The activity that you're experiencing? Do you want to tell us more?"

"Oh, yeah." I glance at LuAnn and she's still looking at me. Scratch that. Into me. It's unnerving. I take a sip of coffee and feel all eyes are on me. "Well, uh, like I said, last night, I woke up with these." I pull up my sleeve again and look at LuAnn.

She seems unimpressed. She just sits there staring at me. *God. What's with this lady?*

"Well," I continue, suddenly feeling like maybe I've wasted everyone's time. "One night there were about six or seven spirits, maybe more, that visited my bedroom and went crazy. I mean, things were moving, *I* was moving… I mean levitated…right off the bed. But then this one spirit showed up, this old lady," I try to stop those two words, *old lady*, from coming out of my mouth for LuAnn's sake, but it was too late, "uh, I mean, like my grandma…I mean, literally, I think it was my great-great grandma. She sort of held me down. I don't really know how to explain it."

LuAnn closes her eyes and leans back. She starts nodding her head slowly. We all just sit there for a moment. LuAnn takes a deep breath in. I glance at Kat. "What else?" LuAnn asks. Her eyes are open again.

What else? Is this lady nuts? Like that wasn't enough? "Well…" There's tons more. Where do I begin?

Then Jason chimes in. "How old were you when you had your first experience, Matty?"

I have to think about that for a minute. "Um…like…three?"

"Three?!?" LuAnn says. She waves her hand at me, "Impossible."

Jason says, "Wow. Three. Generally, people don't realize they're psychic until they're in their teens."

I push back from the table, "Whoa. I didn't say I was psychic. I just said I had my first experience when I was three."

LuAnn lets out a big huff. I swear my hair even moves!

"Seriously. It was Mr. Winston. He was this old guy that played in the backyard with me."

"I thought you said none of them interacted with you like that," Kat says.

"I forgot about him…he was nice. He was like a grandpa. He pushed me on the swings and talked to me while I played in the sandbox."

"How do you know he wasn't a neighbor?" Jason asks.

"Because I took him in the house to meet Mom one day.

I stood there holding his hand. Mom didn't even greet him or anything. She just told me that maybe it was time for her to call some kid down the street and see if they wanted to come and play."

"And then she called the police," LuAnn laughs as she nudges Jason's arm. "Hello? Officer? My child is being stalked by a neighbor."

Ha ha. I don't like the attitude of this LuAnn lady. What's her deal anyway?

I think Jason could see this is going nowhere fast. "So, why don't you tell us about your most recent experience." He looks down at a notepad and scribbles some things. Just like the psychologist I worked with. I'm starting to think this is all a huge mistake.

When I went to the psychologist, she told me I was experiencing a poltergeist syndrome. Basically, I was manifesting this energy in the house because of something deep inside of me. She almost had me convinced. But I read some books about poltergeists, and that's not what this is. I'm just waiting for Jason or LuAnn to use that word, poltergeist, and when they do, I'm outta here.

Then Kat grabs my hand. "It's okay." Her reassurance makes me melt.

I hesitate, then start in. "Well, last night, I was in bed." I don't know why, but I wait for loony LuAnn to crack a joke. The old crackpot. But she just listens and stares at me. "And, well, round one came at about one a.m. It was the one I call the corner ghost. He just kind of stands in the corner and stares, but not in a creepy way, more like in a Boo Radley way."

"I'd call that creepy." Jason mutters as he jots notes down in a small wire-bound notebook.

"Who's Boo Radley?" Kat asks.

"You know, from *To Kill a Mockingbird*? The guy that lives next door."

"Oh yeah. He is creepy."

"No, he's not. Remember at the end how he saves Jem and Scout and he's like this really shy guy—"

"That's enough of the book report girls," LuAnn looks at her dainty silver watch. "Can we move this along?"

Sheesh. Sorry. "Anyway, when I see him, I usually say

something and then he kind of goes away, but I know he's still there. It's like his spirit blushes in reverse; instead of brightening, it disappears." The whole table looks at me quizzically. "So, last night I said, 'Hey Arthur, I see you.' And he just kind of faded out and then he showed up brighter again and then disappeared again. But I knew he was still in the room."

"Why do you call him Arthur?" Jason looks up from his notebook.

"That was Boo Radley's real name."

"Oh," Jason sounds disappointed.

"So, then I just fell asleep while he was there. He doesn't usually do anything but stand in the corner."

"Residual." LuAnn dismisses.

What is with this lady? I know what she means, but this spirit does not seem residual to me. She thinks he's just trapped energy. As if he lived there a long time ago and stood in the corner a lot. Now the house plays that scene every night like a movie. It's not his *spirit*, it's just this *energy*. There's no intelligence behind the ghost. So, he can't communicate because he's not a spirit, he's just a memory.

LuAnn yawns in an exaggerated way. Jason keeps writing.

"Then I fell back to sleep but woke up when I felt the burning on my arm. I sat up in bed and saw a dark shadow move along the foot of the bed." I thought this would impress both of them, but Jason keeps writing and LuAnn just keeps staring, expressionless.

I don't know, this makes me kind of mad. Not at Jason, but LuAnn. Who does she think she is? I don't have to impress her. "Kat. I think we should go." I stand up and Kat looks up at me, stunned.

"What?"

"I don't like the vibe here, that's all."

"But—"

"Come on." I turn and start walking away.

"She means she doesn't like my attitude." LuAnn's all-knowing superior tone is like fingernails on a chalkboard. I can almost feel her judging eyes boring into me as she says it.

I keep walking. I don't want to give her the satisfaction.

"Hey, Matty…" I can hear Jason closing up behind me. He grabs my arm and spins me around.

I feel like I'm just going to go off on him. I'm going to tell him to leave me the frick alone; that I don't want any of this. But once my body spins a 180, and Jason's grip is released on my arm, there's nothing but air in front of me. Jason's nowhere in sight.

That is, until I look back toward the table and see Kat and LuAnn sitting there looking at me. With Jason sitting right between them, writing furiously in his notebook.

By the time I get home, I'm exhausted. I collapse into my bed and feel like I could sleep for a week. I never did tell Jason and crazy LuAnn, or even Kat for that matter, about the Jason-spinning-me-around-but-not-being-there incident. But I did go back to the table and finish the conversation with Jason and crazy lady.

Jason wanted to come over to my house with his full spectrum video camera to record me in my room. That just sounded weird to me. Plus, how would I tell my parents that, one, I had talked to a ghost hunter, and, two, that he was coming over to record me in my bedroom? Uh-uh. No way.

Instead, Jason wants me to go onsite with him and his crew. So, Saturday night Kat and I are going back to Omaha for some overnight ghost hunting at an abandoned convent. I tell my mom and dad that I'm staying over at Kat's house. I wonder what they think about their lesbian daughter staying overnight at a girl's house; but somehow that's a more acceptable thought to them than me connecting with ghosts.

Kat and I follow the phone GPS to the heart of Omaha. The scene at the abandoned convent looks like something out of a ghost hunting show, or Scooby Doo. A beat-up van sits with its back doors open. Orange extension cords stream out of the back of the van like a giant twisted rope. A generator loudly vibrates nearby. Jason and LuAnn are nowhere in sight, but there are two women— one inside the van and one outside—unloading equipment or something.

The double doors of the convent are open wide and the cement walls on either side of the stairs going up to those doors are like arms reaching out, inviting us in. The sun is setting behind us and the windows of the convent are glowing orange from the reflection. The whole building looks like some giant, freaky beast from the middle ages.

"I didn't even know there was a convent here…" I whisper to Kat.

"I know, kinda freaky cool, isn't it?"

I swallow the dryness back into my throat. "Yeah." But I can just imagine what might happen here. I mean, the spirits are all over me in normal life; what's going to happen when I walk into this place?

Kat walks toward the van and I suddenly feel an ice-cold hand on my shoulder. "Are you catholic?" a breath brushes across my ear. My head shoots around so fast, I think I pulled a muscle in my neck.

"Shit! I mean crap…LuAnn, you scared the sh—you scared me!"

She just smiles that weird smile of hers and then walks toward the convent. Geez, that lady freaks me out!

I catch up to Kat and look back at the convent. LuAnn has already disappeared inside.

"Hey Matty, I'm Amber," one of the women extends her hand out to me. She has a friendly smile. She's a little taller than me, maybe 5'7". She must be, like, thirty years old, but I already like her.

"I'm Sara." A woman calls from inside the van. She pronounces her name "Sada," like how we pronounce it in Spanish class. She gives me a little wave. She's a little younger than Amber.

"Hey."

"So, I was just going over things with Kat," Amber's red hair is pulled back in a ponytail. "The most important thing is to stay with one of us and stay calm. If you see anything, hear anything—don't freak out. That's rule number one. Got it?"

"Yeah." I suddenly wonder what I was thinking agreeing to come here. It's not like I have to hunt ghosts; they pretty much hunt me.

"You'll each have a walkie talkie, just in case you get separated. But like I said, stay close."

She hands us the walkie talkies and then gives us instructions on equipment to set up. Mostly we're just running some cords into certain parts of the convent. "Kat, you take this cord into the sanctuary. Matty, you take this one down to the morgue."

"Morgue?" I squeak out.

"Yeah. Take a right when you get inside, you'll go down a long hall. The doors are open to a ramp. At the bottom of the ramp is the morgue."

"Alone?" I whisper/whine.

"Yeah. Just drop the cord and come back up. No big deal. You won't be there long."

"Uh…" I wonder if Amber knows about my track record of seeing. "I…well…"

"She tends to be followed by spirits," Kat interrupts my mumblings. "They find her instead of her finding them."

Amber quickly eyes me up and down.

"Are you psychic?"

"I don't know."

"Hmm." I don't think Amber knows what to think of me. Heck, I don't know what to think of me. "Okay. Kat you take the morgue; Matty you take the sanctuary. You want to run the power cords along the wall so no one trips. Got it?"

This is the first time I've sensed any fear from Kat; she kind of looks like a deer in the headlights.

"Can we go together?" I ask. "I mean, it is our first time setting things up and two heads are better than one." At least that sounded better than "the morgue scares the crap out of us."

Amber looks off to the horizon and takes in a deep breath. "Okay, but don't screw around. We're losing daylight and need to get started soon. Got it?" Amber raises her finger like she's scolding us. "No screwing around. Get the cords down and get back here."

I like her, though. She's not condescending like LuAnn. Amber is firm, but at least we know what she expects from us.

"Yeah. Got it," I say confidently to match her firm tone.

Kat and I each grab a power cord and walk into the mouth of the convent.

"Hello?" Kat's voice echoes back to us in the big open room. I hope to God no one says hello back.

I clutch the orange electrical cord to my chest as Kat grabs my hand. Her hand is soft and smooth and warm. It distracts me from our task for just a minute.

"It's okay," she tries to reassure me.

As I scan the room I see some little closet things off beyond Kat's shoulder. "What's that?"

"Confessionals."

"Like in the movies?" I've never seen confessionals before. I pull her hand and walk toward them. They look just like they do in the movies too. A big closet divided in half by a wall with a little screen kind of thing. I step into one side. "Tell me your secrets," I whisper to Kat.

She just smiles and walks toward the back of the room. "Sanctuary." She's looking through the doorway that leads into another room. "This is where we're supposed to drop the cords."

I grab her hand again and stare into the room. I feel more comfortable now, but I want to hold her hand. Thankfully, she doesn't seem to mind. My heart skips a beat.

We cross the threshold and stand in the giant space. There are rows of wooden pews with those kneeling things, but some of the rows are missing like broken teeth. Pillars hold up the balcony that surrounds the floor of the sanctuary. In front of us is a bare stage with one lone lectern rising from the floor.

"Okay. Let's get this cord down," Kat says.

We work together quickly. She gets on her knees and places the cord while I rip off strips of duct tape and hand them to her. We run the cord along the wall and out the back of the sanctuary just like Amber told us to. There's enough cord to run all the way out to a generator by the van, but we just leave the coiled cord in the entranceway for now.

Kat takes a deep breath. "Now the mortuary."

"Yeah," I manage to gasp out. My mouth is dry as I stare down the long hallway to the right. I see the double doors at the end of the hallway.

"Are you okay?" Kat asks. "Have you seen anyone?"

"No, no." And I haven't. I haven't seen a soul yet, which seems strange.

"Okay, let's go."

Kat grabs my hand again. This time I lean into her. If I could jump into her arms I would. I'm gripping the orange cord so tight, my fingers are starting to hurt.

As we go down the long, wide hallway, the light is starting to fade. There are windows on one side of the hallway, but they have that ripply kind of glass on them. You can't see through them, but you can see light and some vague colors from the outside world: greens and the blue of the sky. I feel like the Cowardly Lion walking to see the Great and Powerful Oz; my knees are shaking.

Just then I feel a whoosh come up behind me and then past me.

"Did you feel that?!?" I ask Kat.

"Like someone just ran past and got ahead of us." She sounds as scared as I feel. "Crap."

I hold her hand tighter. "It'll be okay," I whisper. "Let's just get this cord down and get back out to the van."

I think Kat nods, but I have my eyes on the double doors that are now in front of us. Wooden and thick and old. There's a bar across them. I lift it and the doors swing open. A strong musty air hits us, as if the morgue is gasping for fresh air.

I stifle a cough but then it comes out in a burst.

"Ready?" Kat takes a deep breath and squeezes my hand.

We walk slowly down the incline toward the basement. It suddenly occurs to me that this ramp/driveway kind of thing is here so they could roll bodies down into the basement. Then it occurs to me that nuns died here and they were the ones to be rolled down. I swallow hard.

"How are we supposed to see anything?" I whisper to Kat. Each step we take is going deeper into darkness.

"Oh yeah!" Kat yell-whispers back. There's a click and a beam of light comes out of the flashlight in her hand. "Amber gave it to me."

As she moves the light from left to right, I see in front of us a bunch of deep holes in the wall. Like mini caves that lead to nowhere. They're only as deep as a nun might be tall. There are a dozen of them. Why would twelve nuns die all at once?

We plunge deeper into darkness. The room is dead quiet.

"Where do we run this cord?"

We're almost to the bottom of the ramp.

"I don't know, I guess from the bottom to the top."

We're standing on level ground now and those awful black holes are right in front of us.

Then come the whispers.

Two voices. Two distinct voices.

"Do you hear that?" Kat asks.

I'm glad she did. Usually I'm alone. The hair stands up on the back of my neck.

"Yeah." I can actually hear my heart pounding.

The whispers continue. Like a conversation is going on. And they're getting closer, I swear.

And then I don't know what happens, but Kat is screaming her head off. She's pulling on my hand so hard I take a step back.

And I bump into something.

No wait, someone! Hands grab my arms and I start screaming too.

Kat takes off running to the top of the ramp and I break free from the hands and run as fast as my Chucks will take me. So fast that I catch up to Kat in her Doc Martins and push her out the doors at the top of the ramp.

I stop on the other side of the doors, feeling, maybe wrongly, safe. But Kat keeps running, down the hall, and through the doors. I'm sure she's outside by now.

I don't know what keeps me there, but as soon as one of the doors creeks open, I back away from it.

I see hands. Solid hands. And feet.

And…and…

"Gotcha!!" some random guy yells as he comes out from the doorway.

"Shit!!" I scream back at him. I push him in the chest. "You scared the crap out of us!!"

He and the other random guy laugh hysterically.

I try to be too mad to laugh, but then again, it was pretty funny. And Kat might be all the way back to Fremont by now. "Seriously!" I say, but now I'm laughing too.

"That was classic!" one of the guys says through his laughter.

"Timeless!" the other guy says.

"Creepy!" I yell back at them, joining in the fun, but inside I'm a little pissed off.

"You did well, though," the dark-haired guy says. "I mean, you ran at first, but once you got up here, you actually turned around and faced the door."

"True that," the blond guy says. He looks like a surfer. Tan, blue eyes, floppy bangs. He extends his hand to me. "I'm Troy." He's young, probably 23 or something.

"Matty." I shake his hand. "Nice to feel that you're in solid form, Troy." The minute it leaves my mouth, I realize it sounds like I'm flirting with him. Which I so am not.

"Nunzi," the dark-haired guy says as he holds his hand out to me. "I'm in solid form as well." He might be a year or two younger than Troy.

I laugh as I shake his hand.

"And your friend?" Troy asks.

"That's Jason's cousin, Kat." I look back at the doorway at the end of the hallway. I half-expect Kat to come back, but I guess she's out there getting CPR or something. I realize I'm still clutching the orange cord to my chest. "So, do you need this dropped down in the morgue?" Please, please, please let the answer be no.

"Nah," Nunzi says. "We already dropped line down there about an hour ago. We're good." He gets a little glint in his eye. "But maybe you want to investigate down there with me tonight?"

I can't tell if he's flirting with me or not, but I think he's just toying with me. Either way, have I got a surprise for him. "Sure.

Let's do it." Yeah, I'm as scared as the next gal, but what the heck, dead people visit me whether I'm in a morgue or not.

"Brave girl," Troy says. "Brave girl."

We head outside and catch up with Kat. When she sees Nunzi and Troy for the first time her eyes light up. She playfully slaps Nunzi's shoulder.

I feel a pang of jealousy rise up inside me. I mean, I admit it, Nunzi is cute. Dark skin, dark eyes, curly black hair. And a good body to boot. But Kat, well, she's my…friend… girl…person.

"Scared the crap out of me!" Kat is giggling. Since when does a brooding girl like her giggle?

"You should have seen how fast you ran!"

"I didn't run," Kat protests. "I walked really really fast." Another giggle.

Sheesh.

"Okay, guys and gals, enough goofing around," Amber yells from her perch at the back of the truck. She seems very businesslike when it comes to investigating. "We're all set up. Nunzi and Troy, you take the K2. Kat and—" Amber clicks her fingers, trying to remember my name.

"Matty."

"Yeah, Matty. You and Kat take the digital voice recorders. Guys, show them how to use those. Nunzi and Kat—"

"Can I be with Matty?" Nunzi asks. "She said she wanted to investigate in the morgue. I think she'd be good at that."

I see Kat's whole body exhale air. She deflated right in front of my eyes! I try to send her a look like "sorry," but then I realize I'm not sorry. I want her to be as far away from Nunzi as possible.

"Wow. Matty, starting in the morgue, huh?" Amber says. "Is this for-real ghost hunting stuff, or are you sweet on Nunzi?"

Everyone laughs at that.

"No…I…" How do I even explain it?

Kat is stewing right now. Then she blurts it out. "Matty's not into guys."

I can't believe she just said it. Out loud. In front of everyone. I swallow hard.

"That's cool," Troy says.

Nunzi doesn't look so sure. "Yeah, that's cool."

"Okay, Jason's running late, but let's get started," Amber just kind of moves on. "Troy and Kat, you start in the sanctuary."

The walk down the hallway to the morgue doors is even longer in the dark. Nunzi and I only have our flashlights for light.

I walk cautiously but Nunzi is full steam ahead. He walks like he's running from ghosts, not to them.

"So how did you end up here?" Nunzi asks.

I'm so stupid, I say, "We drove."

Nunzi stops and turns his flashlight on my face for a second, then moves it away. He rephrases his question with a softer voice, "Why did you decide to try ghost hunting?"

"Uh…" that's a good question. *How did I get here?* I was looking for help getting rid of the ghosts, not hunting them.

"I met with Jason and LuAnn."

"LuAnn?"

"Yeah. That psychic lady."

Nunzi pushes open the door to the morgue and that same cool, musty air hits my face. "Are you ready?" he half whispers.

"Yeah." I take a deep breath and end up with a lungful of that cool, musty air. I exhale it.

We walk down the ramp and the air even gets cooler. Nunzi shines his light on the K2 meter.

"What is that?"

"The K2?"

"Yeah."

"It tells us if there are any spikes in the electromagnetic field. If there are, it could be a sign that a ghost is in the room. Or that there's something charging the room with energy." He aims the K2 meter into the air. "Point-one," he says as if I know what that means.

"Is that good?"

"Point-one is our baseline reading. So if it starts to spike, we know it's spiking."

"Okay." I act like I know what he's talking about.

"Do you want to talk?"

Wow. This guy doesn't waste any time. I just met him an hour ago and he wants to have a heart to heart? In a morgue?

"Uh… Kat is right. I'm into girls."

He flashes the light in my eyes again. I can't see his face when he says, "Do you want to talk to the ghosts? Try to get some EVPs?" He must see the blank look on my face. "EVP means electronic voice phenomena."

"Oh…yeah…yeah. That would be great." Luckily, he moved the flashlight before I felt my face turn beet red.

I turn my flashlight onto the digital voice recorder, aka DVR, and hit the play button. Then I stand there with Nunzi. For a while.

"Do you want me to start?" Nunzi is starting to sound annoyed. What does he expect? This is my first investigation.

"Uh…"

Then he jumps right in. "Is there anyone here with us tonight?"

Nunzi's light flashed from wall to wall as we ran down the long hallway. I could hear him breathing hard. My flashlight was laying on the floor of the morgue, but I wasn't going back to get it.

"What was that?!?" he's yelling, breathless.

I run into the back of him. He isn't moving and I try to push him.

"The door—" he's fighting for air. "It won't open!"

I push past him and push onto the door. It opens instantly.

"It wouldn't open!" he yells as we run through the front hallway and out the front door.

Amber is waiting for us at the back of the van when we get outside. "What happened?" She seems half-panicked, half-angry.

Nunzi starts telling the story, breathlessly, "We were doing an EVP session. Usual questions. This hand grabbed my shoulder. I thought it was her," he points at me. "But it wasn't. She was there," he motions to open air in front of him. "I turned and flashed my light and it was this woman."

"And man," I add.

"There was a man?"

I nod. He didn't see the man? He was scarier than the woman.

"The woman raised her chin," Nunzi continues. "Like this." He raises his chin up in the air but his eyes are on Amber. "And she—" Nunzi turns and starts gagging.

"Her throat was slashed," I jump in. "From here to here." I draw my finger across my throat. It was a big gash. "We could see the bone and blood and stuff." I don't know what that stuff in the human neck is called. Nunzi makes a heaving sound.

Nunzi composes himself quickly and adds, "She made this sound," and he tries to recreate it, but it was unworldly, or otherworldly. "It was like a gurgling breath. Like she was trying to talk but blood got in the way."

"Did you catch it on the dvr?" Amber asks.

Nunzi grabs the recorder from me and fumbles around to rewind it.

"Then the man grabbed the woman and pulled her back into the shadows," I say.

"I didn't see the guy," Nunzi says as he's looking at the recorder. He hits a button and the recorder starts to play.

We can hear our voices asking questions and then some rustling. Nunzi holds up his finger and whispers, "Here…"

We can hear Nunzi gasp and I said, "What…?" then "Oh my God!"

Then we hear the horrible rasping, gasping sound of the woman. Next my flashlight drops and then we hear our footsteps running.

Nunzi almost turns off the recorder when we hear a raspy female voice say "heeeeeelp."

More fumbling, Nunzi saying "The door—it won't open!"

Nunzi shuts off the recorder.

Amber says, "We have to go back in!" She grabs her flashlight from inside the van.

Nunzi and I look at each other in shocked silence. Amber pushes past us and Nunzi finally says, "Why are we going back in?!?"

I agree with Nunzi, but then my voice comes out without even thinking, "We need to get more people to go in with us. Like Sara and Troy or something. We can't go in just the three of us."

Amber asks Sara where Jason is; he evidently got here when we were inside. Amber gets on the walkie talkie. "Jason, Troy, I need you to come to the van. NOW!"

Both Jason and Troy acknowledge Amber with a quick "copy" through the walkie talkie.

While we wait for them to join us, Amber rests back on the van. She runs her flashlight across my and Nunzi's faces. "You both look pale. Are you okay?"

We both answer with a feeble yes, but I think Nunzi is doing a bit less okay than I.

"So did you get a good look at the guy? The one that pulled the lady back."

Nunzi again says that he didn't see the guy. I tell Amber that all I could see was a shadow. A tall shadow. "It was big."

"Do you guys think this was real? I mean, should we call the cops?"

"Seemed real to me," Nunzi says.

I hate to contradict but it just comes out, "The lady was kind of glowing, though. I mean not glowing bright, but there was a halo of light around her. And how could she live with her throat slit like that?"

Amber looks to Nunzi. He thinks for a moment before saying, "Good point."

"What's up?" Jason's voice from behind us nearly makes me jump out of my shoes.

Amber catches Jason up to speed, with a few interjections from Nunzi and me. Kat squeezes my shoulder in a reassuring way from time to time. Jason just kind of nods throughout the story, but Amber seems to come to a panic as the story is laid out again. "Do you think we should call the police?" she asks.

"We have a camera in the morgue, right? Have you checked the monitors? Replayed what happened?" Jason asks.

"Crap. I was so worried that one of them was going to pass out…" Amber jumps into the back of the van and everyone follows. "Sara, anything on the video?"

"Not that I can see, but it's cued up."

Sara plays the recording. We can see Nunzi's flashlight snap around, then I drop my flashlight and Nunzi and I run. "I don't see anything," Amber says.

"Rewind it," Jason instructs.

We watch it again in slow motion. And again. And again.

"There!" Jason says and points to Nunzi's shoulder on the screen.

Amber isolates those pixels and enlarges the screen.

"See," Jason says, "The fabric of his sleeve is crumpled. Like someone's holding it like this." Jason clutches Nunzi's sleeve in his fist.

"Oh yeah," Kat whispers beside me.

I see it too. Amber points to the same place on the screen.

Nunzi and I both agree. "But why can't we see her hand, or her arm?" I ask. "And how come we saw her so clearly?"

"Well, we know one thing for sure," Jason says, "This wasn't something being played out."

"So, not residual?" Nunzi asks.

"Hard to know," Jason says.

"But we have the EVP of the woman saying 'help,'" I add.

"You have an EVP?"

"Oh yeah, sorry Jase." Amber picks up the recorder and plays the EVP.

"Hmmm," Jason scratches his chin. "Again, hard to say if it's residual or not. That could be her interacting, but it could be part of the residual haunt." He looks at both of us. "Do you guys want to go back down there?"

Nunzi and I answer together, but with opposite answers. Nunzi says "no," but I say "yes."

I'm not in the morgue. I'm in a long hallway in the dorm wing. Amber and Jason didn't think it would be good for me to go into the morgue again. So Kat went down to the morgue with Nunzi and Jason, and I was sent upstairs with Troy.

Troy's flashlight bounces off the corners of the ceiling. "It's cold in here," he says.

"Yeah." I half-heartedly shine my flashlight in different corners of the room. I don't know why I feel so crabby about it; I really didn't need to go back into the morgue. Although I have to admit I'm jealous that Kat is with Nunzi. At least Jason is there to make sure nothing happens between them.

Troy steps out into the hallway for a minute, then comes back in. He must be recording because the little red light is glowing on the digital recorder.

"Is there anyone in here with us?" he asks. He turns his back to me. "Would you like to talk with us?"

His flashlight runs past the doorway and I gasp.

I saw her clear as day. A black robe, a white collar, a mournful gaze.

I don't say anything though.

I aim my beam toward the doorway and there's nothing there. I know I saw her.

Then a cold hand grasps my shoulder and squeezes.

"Uh…Troy."

A voice as human as anyone living is right next to my ear. Her voice is raspy, strained, and, well, gurgly, like she has blood or something in the way. It's the same "help" we heard down in the morgue.

"Troy!"

His flashlight turns toward me. "Matty?"

"Do you see her?"

"Who?"

He has to see her. His flashlight is exactly aimed toward me. I can hear her gurgled breaths next to my ear. I can feel each ice-cold finger on my shoulder blade.

"You don't see anything?" My voice cracks because my throat is bone dry. I swallow hard. "Behind me…to the right."

His flashlight roams all around me. "No. What is it?"

"EVP," I say and beckon him with my left hand to come forward.

The woman's breathing is getting faster and shorter. She's nearly gasping. And the gurgling is like a pot of boiling soup.

Goose bumps rise up my legs, my torso, and over my arms.

The air is thick.

He puts the dvr right in front of me. "It's freezing over here," he whispers. "All around you; it's, like, ten degrees colder here."

I don't say anything.

"Who's here with us?" Troy says.

I can hear the gurgling turn into gasping, like she's trying to say something, and then just a weak "help."

Then it all stops.

There's no more breathing, rasping, or gurgling. There's just silence. The grip on my shoulder has been released.

"She's gone," I say.

"What was it, Matty?" Troy's still whispering. He holds his flashlight under his chin so I can see him talking.

I raise my flashlight under my chin. "A nun. It's the same spirit from the morgue."

"For real?"

I shake my head and light beams move around me. "I saw

her in the doorway. Just a flash when you aimed your light that way. I didn't realize it when I saw her downstairs, but she was a nun. She wore a habit, but without the hood thingie." I inhale, then say, "So I could see…" I run my finger across my throat.

"Shit," Troy gasps.

"Then she was behind me, asking for help." I swallow hard again as the goose bumps roll across my entire body.

"Let's get out of here," Troy whispers.

I don't argue.

The whole team is waiting next to the van when Troy and I go outside. A cool breeze floats across my back and the goose bumps rise again. Or maybe it's because Kat is standing next to me, so close I can smell her woodsy kind of hair product. I breathe in a big whiff.

"What did you see?" She whispers in my ear, so close I can feel her breath on my earlobe.

Oh crap. I take a deep breath and count slowly to ten. That trick my psychologist taught me works when cute girls are whispering in my ear too.

Amber and Jason are standing inside the van giving instructions on how we need to break down. Basically, we roll everything up and load it neatly into the van. Kat and I decide we'll work together on the breakdown, but Amber told us not to go into the morgue. Everywhere else was fine, though.

Before we go back in to get the equipment, Amber asks if she can talk to me for a minute. She sits at the back of the van, her legs dangling below her. "Jason tells me that you've had some pretty intense experiences, like, since you were little."

I have a moment of wanting to run, thinking maybe she wants to send me to therapy or discount everything I told Jason by saying that I was dreaming or something. Or maybe she'll use that poltergeist thing on me, but then she says, "I think you're psychic."

That takes me by surprise. "Huh?" It's all I can manage to get out.

"I think," Amber jumps out of the back of the truck and grabs both of my hands in hers. "You're psychic."

"You mean like LuAnn?" I ask.

"Who's LuAnn?" she says.

"That weird lady…" Well, maybe Amber is friends with that creepy creep. "That elderly woman I met when we had coffee with Jason."

Amber has a confused look on her face but continues. "Matty, Jason said this has been going on since you were three or four. Is that right?"

"Yeah," I look at the ground.

"And what you saw in there tonight."

"Nunzi saw it too!" My voice whines even though I don't want it to.

"I mean in the bedroom, upstairs. Troy didn't see it."

"He just wasn't looking. He was looking at the K2 or something." The K2 is that electromagnetic field detector (EMF). Even though it picks up vibes most people can't feel, I didn't need a K2 meter to tell me anything.

Now, Amber shakes her head. "We looked back at the recording. There was nothing. I mean, nothing we could see. But you clearly did see it."

"But it was dark in there." I'm reaching a panic state now. Will she call my mom and tell her everything? Will I have to go back into counseling? Or maybe I'll be put into a psyche ward or something. I feel like I might cry.

"Matty…" When Amber squeezes my hand, I realize that she's still holding both of my hands in hers. I suddenly feel uncomfortable. "Our cameras have IR technology—infrared— they can see in the dark. We can pick up shapes, movement, haze, whatever. There was nothing there."

"Maybe I imagined it?" What she's saying just can't be. "I mean, Nunzi and I both saw it in the morgue, right? And we didn't notice she was a nun there. So maybe I just imagined seeing her as a nun upstairs. Maybe my mind was playing tricks on me."

Amber releases her grip on my shoulder. "And all the other apparitions you've seen? Are they just your imagination too?"

"My psychologist says—"

"Forget your psychologist. You're not crazy, Matty. You're psychic. I'm telling you."

I gulp. Hard. Could Amber be right? My eyes are fixed on the gravel beneath us as my mind reels. Psychic? Me? I don't want to be psychic. I don't want to be anything. I just want to be Matty, who goes to high school and has some friends and maybe meets a nice girl. Psychics are weird. Like LuAnn.

"Matty." Amber pulls on my chin so that I'm looking her in the eye. "This is a gift."

Even though she's being very motherly in her approach to all this, I feel a whoosh of anger rise inside me and I pull my chin from her grasp. "A gift?" I try to keep my voice down, but it gets away from me. Blood rushes into my face. "My parents think I'm crazy. My sister hates me because we had to move. And these stupid ghost people visit me all the time. In class. At home. When I'm sleeping. When I'm awake." My voice rises to a higher pitch as if to put an exclamation point on every word that comes out of my mouth. I just want it all to go away. To just freaking go away.

"Matty." There she goes, holding both of my hands again, being all motherly and teacherly and all. I try to pull my hands away from her, but she only squeezes tighter. "It's just that you don't know how to control it yet. These spirits, ghosts, whatever you want to call it, they're reaching out to you. They want your help."

"My help? What can I do for them? I go to freaking high school. I don't even know how to help myself."

"They don't know that. They see you as a kind of beacon. A way for them to communicate. A way for them to move on."

"Move on? Like, to heaven?"

"Heaven, another realm, whatever."

"But psychics are…weird. Look at that lady from Poltergeist with the squeaky shoes. And LuAnn. I don't want to be a weird psychic lady."

"Okay. I don't know who LuAnn is, but that lady from Poltergeist was a Hollywood version of a psychic." Amber lets go of my hands, turns, and leans back on the van. She sighs deeply, like I'm wearing her out or something. But hey…she just called me psychic. This is kinda big. As if she can read my mind she says, "How about 'medium'? Does that term feel better to you?"

I tug on my shirt. "Well, personally I'm a small…"

"Cut the crap," Amber says with a slight smile. "You know what I mean."

"Medium." I roll the word around in my head. "You mean like the *Long Island Medium* lady?"

Amber blows a puff of air out of her mouth, like she's exasperated or something. "Okay. Yeah. Like the *Long Island Medium* lady."

"She's not so bad. I guess."

"Okay. Good. A medium. I think you're a medium."

My mind is spinning with all kinds of thoughts and memories. My parents taking me to a shrink. My schoolmates in Denver making fun of me. The grandpa-type man who went away only to be replaced by some Boo Radley guy who stood in a corner, watching me.

"Matty?" Amber interrupts my thoughts. "Are you okay?"

"No," I say thoughtfully. "I'm not okay."

"Have you ever talked to any of them?"

"Talked…?" Medium, medium, medium drums in my head so that I can't even comprehend what Amber's asking.

"Have they ever talked to you?"

I think back over all the people—ghosts—spirits—whatever. I mean, what does a medium call them? Can I go to medium school? I think about them and I can't ever remember them talking to me. "I don't think so."

"Have you ever tried talking to them?"

Kat suddenly appears behind Amber running her fingers through her long bangs again, looking all hot and shit. Then she points at her watch. I look at my watch and see that it's 1:00 a.m. "Shit, I mean, sorry, shoot, I've gotta go. My parents think I'm at Kat's and…" Oh no, what did I just say? I try to cover my tracks quick, "Well, it's not like they're awake, but if they were and they knew we were driving home this late, well, you know…" I pass by Amber and walk quickly toward Kat.

"Your parents don't know you're here?!" Amber yells behind me.

"It's all okay!" I yell back, but it really isn't.

"Matty!" Amber yells louder as I get closer to Kat. "Try talking to them!"

I don't turn around or even acknowledge that I've heard her. I just keep walking with Kat back to the car.

"What was that all about?" Kat asks. I can feel Amber's eyes boring holes in the back of my head. I wonder if that's a medium thing too.

"Nothing. She just wanted to ask me some questions about the nun with the slashed throat." Remembering the nun sends chills down my spine. I shudder.

"She was a nun?" Kat asks.

"Yeah. Which makes it all the more creepy, doesn't it?" I don't really want to talk about this because what if I did imagine it. What if I'm wrong?

"Are you okay?" Kat asks.

"Yeah, of course."

"Teacher's pet." Kat bumps her shoulder into mine as we get to the car.

"Not really. I don't think. Do you think?"

We both get in our respective sides of the car and as we fasten our seat belts, Kat says, "Yuh huh," She sounds flirty all the sudden. *Whatev.*

A hand pounds on my window. Kat and I both scream, then start laughing when we realize Amber is standing on the other side of the glass.

I roll down the window. "We're investigating here again next Saturday night if you both want to join us."

I look at Kat and she nods. "Uh, yeah, sure," I say. Better than spending a Saturday night in Fremont.

"But do me a favor and tell your parents, okay?"

I look at Kat and she again nods. "Uh, yeah, of course," I say, but I don't mean it. My parents would kill me if they found out I was doing this…inviting ghosts into my life.

"Okay," Amber pounds her hand on the window frame of the car. "See you next week."

On the drive home I keep thinking about that word— *medium.* What a dumb word. But I guess it's better than psychic.

"So what did Amber talk to you about, really?" Kat breaks the silence.

"She thinks I'm a medium," I blurt out.

"Well, duh."

I glance at Kat, then return my eyes to the road. "What do you mean?"

"Matty. How many people do you know who see so many ghosts? I mean, I see a few here and there, but nothing like you do."

"Yeah, but I don't talk to them. They don't talk to me."

"I thought that grandpa guy talked to you when you were little."

I think about that. She's right. He did. Then there was a little girl once, in my bedroom, late at night. I was seeing the shrink back then. I even told her about the little girl and how she sang songs in another language or something. The shrink told me that my imagination was getting away with me and maybe I should become a writer. I wonder what she would say if I told her I was a medium.

"Did you know that Nunzi is getting a parapsychology degree at the U? " Kat says. She's talking so fast it sounds like maybe she drank too much coffee at the van. "And Troy wants his own ghost hunting show? He stayed overnight at the Villisca Murder House once." Then she goes on to explain that the house is in a small Iowa town and these murders happened there in the 1800s and it's haunted as hell. Then she comes back to the case at hand, "Was that nun scary?"

"Well, yeah, I mean, she had a slashed throat and she was making this gurgling kind of sound."

"See! She was trying to talk to you."

"Talk? I don't know." But there was that rasping, gurgling sound. And the "help." I open my window a crack to get some fresh air.

"I wonder if a nun got murdered there or something. I mean, I wonder what the history of the place is?"

"Amber and Jason must know. Right? I mean, I would think."

"Let's ask them tomorrow. But you'd think they would have told us."

"Yeah."

As Kat keeps talking on at rapid speed, I think about all that's happened before and all that's happening now. The woman at the foot of my bed, who seems to be my great-grandma; the young girl who keeps popping up when I least expect her; the Boo Radley guy who appeared for several years in the corner of my room, quietly watching me. Then I think about something else. I start to put the pieces together. What Amber said, what Jason and Nunzi said. My heart starts pounding in my chest and I yell out, "LuAnn!!"

I yell it so loud that it stops Kat's monologue instantly. "What?" she asks.

"LuAnn." I say it again, and one more time for good measure. "LuAnn."

"What are you talking about?"

"That lady…LuAnn. She met us for coffee."

"Us?"

"Yeah. She was with Jason."

"What are you talking about?"

I knew it! I should have known it before! Just for confirmation, I say, "When we met Jason at the coffeeshop, there was a lady with him. An elderly lady with white hair and she was kind of creepy. She sat right next to you."

I pull into a gas station that's halfway between Omaha and Fremont and put the car in park. I look right at Kat and say, "LuAnn. LuAnn."

"What are you talking about, Matty? There was only me, you, and Jason."

I nod my head. The hair on the back of my neck bristles.

"Me, you, Jason…" I say, "And a ghost named LuAnn."

7

I can't focus on school the whole next week. I just keep thinking about the team, and the nun, and how this is the most excited I've felt in a long time. I don't even mind the ghosts that show up here and there during my day. I can't wait to tell Amber about LuAnn and how I've realized she's not real. It's going to blow her mind.

I don't go to the front of the school these mornings to hang out with Angie and Emily. I go directly behind the school to find Kat. She's always there with her headphones over her head, but, I don't know, sometimes it seems like she's waiting for me.

The week is going so slowly. It's only Wednesday and I feel like Saturday will never get here. It doesn't help that my parents are missing in action. Mom and Dad landed some big case and they've been working late. Dad has to go to San Francisco tomorrow for a deposition or something and Mom has to do some muckity muck thing with the client; she said she might have to spend some nights at a hotel in Omaha. Bottom line: Sasha and I are pretty much on our own for awhile. "We trust you guys to take care of yourselves," Mom says. Which means, "We trust that you won't have any parties."

The only party I could be having is with the ghosts in the basement.

Kat takes off her headphones when I tap her on the shoulder.

"Happy *Cinco de Mayo*," I say.

"Huh?" Kat looks like she's half-asleep.

"It's *Cinco de Mayo*, the 5th of May."

"Oh yeah," Kat says. "Hey."

I sit down next to her and she rests her head on my shoulder. Her hair tickles my neck. Ummm, okay. I don't move. And I don't know what to say.

We sit like that for what seems like an eternity, and now I'm starting to feel uncomfortable. Did she fall asleep?

"Tired?" I finally say.

"What?" Kat doesn't move her head.

"Tired?" I repeat.

"Yeah." She doesn't move.

Okay. Well, I guess this is just how we're sitting here this morning.

"Have you talked to Jason this week?"

"Huh?"

What the heck? Am I not speaking clearly, or loud enough, or something?

"Have you talked with Jason this week?"

"Jason? No."

"Are you okay?"

"Tired," she says.

Geez. *Give me something here, Kat.*

And then she does. "Do you want to go to prom with me?"

Just like that, out of the blue, Kat asks me.

"What?"

"I was thinking, the guys here are douche bags and stupid, and, I don't know, I think it would be kind of fun to go with you."

"To prom? Like a date?" This girl confuses me so much.

"Like *friends*," she says.

No confusing that.

"Well..." I was kind of thinking of asking this girl in my science class. I'm not sure, but she *might* be... "Do you know Cyn Meyer?"

"Cyn Meyer...Cyn Meyer..."

"She's like 5'7", plays basketball..."

"A jock? Don't know her."

"I'm thinking..."

Kat lifts her head off my shoulder. "You're thinking of asking her to prom?!?"

"Well, yeah, but I don't know..."

Kat sits up. I don't know if she's hurt, jealous, or just thinking.

"I didn't really want to go to prom anyway..." She does look hurt. Well, this is a fine turn of events. I don't know how I feel about it.

We show up at the abandoned convent the next weekend. Kat looks smoking hot in black leggings and a black camisole under a black Ramones t-shirt that hangs off one shoulder. Sigh. I wish she were dressing that way for me, but she talked about Nunzi all the way here.

My mom must think I have quite the thing going with Kat because I told them that I'm staying over at her house again tonight. But Mom is so busy with that big case, she hasn't been home much lately, except to sleep; and Dad is still in San Francisco.

Jason high-fives his cousin Kat and she immediately says, "Matty has an interesting story for you…"

I wasn't really planning on telling Jason first; I kind of wanted to tell Amber. "Oh yeah?"

"Yeah," I say. "But is Amber around? I kind of want her to hear it too."

Jason walks us over to the van. If Jason and Kat didn't act like they knew who Amber was, I'd start to think she was some kind of van-ghost. She never seems to be away from the van. "Hey, what's up?" she says as she gets up from her chair in front of the video monitor.

"Okay, so I've mentioned this LuAnn woman a couple of times now—"

"LuAnn?" Jason says.

"Yeah. She was with us at the coffeeshop, when Kat and I first met with you."

Jason looks perplexed.

"Wait 'til you hear this, cous." Kat pokes at Jason.

"Neither of you knows LuAnn, right?"

Jason and Amber look at each other and both respond "no."

"She was even here last weekend. Scared the crap out of me. Right over there, by that tree." I point in the direction where LuAnn walked up behind me. "Well, I figured it out. She's a ghost, spirit, whatever."

"Who is she?" asks Amber.

"That's what I want to know," I say. "She told me she was a psychic, but she's been all creepy and weird toward me. Like she doesn't like me or something. Like she knows more than me and she wants me to know it. Or like I'm invading her turf or something."

Amber seems excited. "Have you talked to her?"

"We've had conversations. Right there in front of Kat and Jason. I guess it all kind of sounded like my answers were part of the conversation with them."

"Spirit guide?" Jason asks Amber.

"Maybe," Amber seems kind of hesitant. "When does she show up?"

I think about that for a minute. "Weird, but, whenever I'm around Jason, pretty much. I mean, she's never shown up any other time."

"*Your* spirit guide?" Amber points to Jason.

"You think she's attached to me?" he asks.

"Could be. Matty only sees her when you're around."

I want to say, *Hey, I'm standing right here*, but instead I say, "Wait…I didn't see Jason yesterday until later in the day, but I saw her right after we got here."

"So, here's what we do. You need to keep track of when you see her and who's around you. She could be your spirit guide, Jason's spirit guide, or something else."

"What's a spirit guide?" asks Kat.

"Just what it sounds like, they watch over us, take care of us, help us through stuff. For a medium," Amber points at me even though I'm not sure I want to wear that term yet, "they can offer protection."

"She doesn't seem like she wants to protect me. More like she wants to watch me fall," I say.

"And while we're on that subject—Matty, you need to learn how to say a prayer of protection. Ask your spirit guides to surround you, especially when you go on an investigation."

"Uh, well, I'm not really religious," I try to say this delicately, hoping I don't offend anyone. "I don't really pray."

"Okay, then," Amber seems a little exasperated. I'm sure that between this and my opposition to using the word psychic, she thinks I'm a little nuts. "How about you just say words of protection?"

"I...I can do that." Who doesn't need protection every now and then?

Jason and Kat go find the other investigators, and I'm sure that Kat is excited to go find Nunzi. Nunzi-this and Nunzi-that. Blah, blah, blah.

Amber asks me to take a seat in the van with her. I watch Kat walk away and I'm torn about where I want to be right now.

Amber grabs my hands and tells me to quiet my mind and focus. How can I quiet my mind when Kat is being flirty with Nunzi? *She's my girl!* I want to yell. But she really isn't.

Amber snaps her fingers to get my attention and says, "Matty, this is serious. You need to really focus here." She takes me through some breathing exercises. At first I feel kind of dumb. But after awhile, it feels good. Like just lying in bed on a spring morning and listening to the birds outside. I know, I'm weird. I like to listen to birds.

We start working on the words of protection, which she's now calling a spell. I can go with that too. So, I learn my spell of protection and Amber tells me how important it is to say these words before I make contact with spirits, ghosts, whatever.

"But sometimes they show up in the middle of the night, or at school—times when I don't expect them."

Amber lets go of my hands and nods her head emphatically.

"You need to say this every night before you go to bed, every morning before you go to school. Whenever you need it most."

Geez. That's going to be all the time. "How long will it hold? I mean, can I say it every two hours? I see ghosts. A lot."

"You can say it whenever you feel the need." Amber grabs my hands again. "The thing is, Matty, you're really vulnerable. The reason you're getting all these visits is because you're an open portal right now. Think of it like a telephone. All these spirits, these beings, who are trapped here for one reason or another have no way to communicate with anyone. Except you. They've discovered that you can hear them, see them. So they want to tell you, or show you, what's wrong and that they need help."

I feel sweat form on my eyebrows. I pull my hands away from Amber and rub my face with both hands. "I don't want this," I manage to say.

Amber hands me a bottle of water. I open it and drink half of it.

"Unfortunately, you don't have a choice. But now that you know what this is, you can do whatever you need to keep yourself protected and safe."

"With these words, this spell, will all of these things stop bothering me?"

Amber sits back in her chair. "No, I'm afraid not." She leans forward again. "But it will keep the bad spirits from seeking you out. You'll still see the spirits seeking help, and it will probably get worse before it gets better, but at least you won't be visited by the beings who are trying to cause harm."

I know Amber's trying to be reassuring, but this isn't helping.

"I should go…" I stand up, but then I think, *go where?* I'm here to investigate. And how am I supposed to help these people? And who are these bad beings anyway. This is too much. It's all just too much. Can't I just be normal for once?

Amber grabs my wrist and pulls me back for one more minute.

"And Matty, that LuAnn, be careful of her, okay?"

"Why?"

"Your instincts about her. They seem like maybe she's not what she says she is. Right?"

"Well...I don't know. She just seems kind of creepy and weird."

"She may be your spirit guide, or she may be Jason's, but she may be something else."

"Something else? Like...what?"

"Well, I don't want to jump to conclusions here, but she may be... well, she may be a demon."

That word echoes around in my head. Demon.

And speaking of demons, Kat shoots me a look when I'm paired with Nunzi for the investigation.

Geez. Talk about worlds colliding—the other world and this world—both of them seem mad at me.

Nunzi and I are sitting in the sanctuary this time. He's sitting on the steps to the stage or whatever they call that thing where the priest stands, and I'm sitting a few feet away on one of the unbroken pews.

"So you're a psychic, huh?" Nunzi says. He's holding the dvr and some other thing that checks rooms temperature.

"I guess." I look up toward the balcony that surrounds this place. I get more spirit action in English Lit.

"And a lesbian."

Wow. Okay, I guess this guy needs to talk.

"Yeah."

"Wild."

"Why?"

"Well, you just…you don't look like a lesbian."

"Huh. What does a lesbian look like?" I'm curious. Maybe I'm doing something wrong.

"I don't know. A truck driver or something. Like, wearing flannel and being overweight."

"Wow. Really?" My sarcasm comes out loud and clear. "What about Ellen and Portia? Or Kristen Stewart?"

He thinks about that for a minute. He doesn't say anything; he just looks down at the instruments in his hands.

Whatever. I keep my eyes on the balcony, but I don't know why. There's nothing going on in here.

"Yeah. You're right."

I look back at Nunzi. "What?"

"I totally stereotyped it. Like people do with me and my family."

I look at him and shine my flashlight on his face.

"We're Mexican."

I don't say anything and instead scan my flashlight across the balcony.

"Sorry," he says.

"No problem."

"Feel anything?"

"Look, Nunzi, you seem like a nice guy and all, but I think Kat is into you. If you're looking for a high school girl to go out with…"

"I mean in the room," Nunzi interrupts. "Is anything here?" His voice echoes off into the high ceilings.

"Oh," I say, "sorry." Crap. I try to quickly recover, "Nah. I don't know if they won't come in here because it's a sanctuary or what, but I don't feel anything."

"Me neither. Let's move into one of those hallways up there." He points his flashlight to a doorway off the balcony.

"Yeah. Sounds good."

We take the back staircase up to the second floor. Nunzi steps onto the balcony and looks down for a minute, as if checking the sanctuary one more time. He then motions me to follow him. The door to the long hallway opens with a loud creak. Nunzi says, "That's us opening the door" just in case any recording devices catch the sound. That was something Amber told us to do when Kat and I first started the investigation the night before. She said that there were cameras and digital recorders in various locations and if we made any noises we should announce it so they knew it wasn't paranormal.

Nunzi and I stand side by side as we aim our flashlights down the long hall. It takes a turn to the right. As we walk down the hallway, I can see that windows line one side of the wall. My knees are kind of shaking, but I don't know why.

At the end of the long hallway, we take the turn and are faced with another long hallway. That's when I feel the pressure start to build in the air. "It's kind of stuffy in here," I whisper. Nunzi doesn't say anything in return. I wonder if he nodded his head or something. As we aim our flashlights down the corridor, I see a bunch of doors lined up like soldiers. It's funny; there's nothing at all scary about this place, really. The walls are a crisp white, the doors are in good shape, and they're all closed. It's as if when they shut down this place, all the nuns got together and closed all the doors at the same time. Then walked single file down the long hallway and out the doors. No attachments. Just moving on.

But the air feels like something else is happening here.

We keep moving. Nunzi is now a few steps ahead of me; he's opening doors and shining his flashlight in every room. I follow by shining my flashlight too.

The air is oppressive. And cold. It's like a January day when you step outside and the cold freezes the hairs in your nose and takes the breath right out of your lungs. I shiver. Nunzi keeps opening doors, shining his light. As I look in a room, I see movement from the corner of my eye. I quickly aim my flashlight behind me and see Amber. She's standing next to a window. She has her finger to her lips begging me to be quiet. She motions for me to come into the room.

I look ahead at Nunzi and see he's still opening doors, oblivious that Amber is here. I'm sure she wants to play some kind of joke on him. I quietly snicker to myself and step into the room with Amber.

She's grinning like the cat that ate the canary. My light reflects off the glass of the window she stands next to. I step into the room and the air is even colder. "God, it's so cold," I whisper. I aim my flashlight up from my chin, "I can even see my breath." A wisp of cold air rises out of my mouth, cutting through the flashlight beam. "What's up?"

I flash the light toward Amber, but she's not there.

BAM! The door slams behind me.

Darn! It's a joke on me, not on Nunzi. My heart pounds in my chest because the air is just so weird in here. I try to take in as much air as I can, but I'm starting to feel dizzy. I go to the door and put my hand on the knob. It's ice cold. So cold it burns. I pull my hand away, wondering what they have in store for me.

"Amber?" I try to keep my voice calm so she knows I'm not scared. Or at least I'm not acting scared, because my heart is in my throat right now. I'm even feeling claustrophobic, like the walls are closing in on me.

I hear a woman laugh from the corner of the room, over by the window, where Amber was standing when I stepped in.

I try the knob again; it's still ice cold, but I'm prepared this time. I turn the knob and it breaks free from my grip and spins. I step back. *How'd they get it to do that?*

"Nunzi?" my voice nearly squeaks, like I'm going to cry. I take a deep breath. This is just some kind of test. I won't panic.

Now voices rise up in the room. Men talking. Women whispering. Their voices come up from the floor and start to spin around the room like a tornado. They're talking so fast, I can't make out what they're saying. I push my back into the wall so no one can sneak up on me. I aim my flashlight to each corner of the room but no one's there. The voices might even be speaking Latin. They chatter rapidly.

The beam of my flashlight is moving back and forth; it's as if I'm trying to track the voices that surround me. Or maybe I'm just looking for some speakers or something.

Then my flashlight dies.

And the voices stop abruptly.

And I think there's no way the team could get my flashlight to cut off at the same time they stop the voices.

I remember what Amber said about the spell of protection and start chanting it rapidly in my head. Then I hear a voice. "Matty?"

It's Nunzi, outside the door to the hallway.

I'm not moving my back away from this wall so I just yell and pound on the door next to me. "Here!"

"Matty?" His voice is on the other side of the door.

"Here!!" I pound harder.

The door swings open and Nunzi's flashlight beam bounces off the window across the room. I dart out of the room so fast Nunzi actually screams and drops his flashlight.

Now we're both in the hallway in pitch black. Nunzi's flashlight beam lays on the floor and is aimed for the far side of the room.

"What happened?!?" Nunzi asks as he steps toward his flashlight. I stand in the hallway and watch, feeling halfway like I want to cling to his arm and follow him in and halfway like I don't.

"Nunzi, wait!" I say, but it's too late. He's already inside the room. My heartbeat pounds in my ears as I wait for the door to slam shut and separate us once again.

But nothing happens. Nunzi picks up his flashlight and returns to the hallway.

"Didn't Amber tell you not to leave your teammate?" Nunzi's voice has raised to scolding schoolteacher pitch.

"Yeah, but I didn't..." And my voice lowers to mumbling student.

"What the hell happened?"

I lay out the story for him, telling him all about how Amber appeared and beckoned me into the room. "I thought we were going to play a joke on you..." My voice is still in that mumbly kind of stage.

"Shape shifter," Nunzi whispers.

"What?"

"Come on," he says and grabs my arm. He's walking so fast he's nearly dragging me. I feel like I'm in major trouble. He doesn't say another word all the way out to the van.

"Amber," he calls out urgently. He still has a grip on my arm. Geez. Put me in handcuffs or something why don't you?

"Tell her your story, Matty." His tone is so authoritative that I think if he had a gun the barrel would be lodged between my shoulder blades right now.

"Well..." I swallow hard. I must really be in trouble. I don't know what I did wrong, but Nunzi is really serious. Amber looks at me with a furrowed brow.

"Nunz?" Amber jumps out of the back of the van.

Nunzi nudges me. POG, that's me, Prisoner of Ghost Hunting.

"I was in the hallway," my voice is almost pleading. I think I'd rather be up against the ghosts than up against these two; I guess I committed the cardinal sin of ghost hunting or something. "And you were there… you called me into a room… I thought we were going to play a joke…" Then I look at Nunzi. "Sorry." Sarcasm drips off the word sorry and I wish I could take it back, so I just repeat it in the right way. "Sorry."

"Wait. What?" Amber looks at Nunzi.

"She's only telling you pieces, wait 'til you hear the whole thing." Nunzi says as he grabs a Coke from a cooler next to the van. His voice filled with excitement.

I relax my shoulders. Maybe I'm not in trouble.

"Tell me, Matty. Don't leave out details this time. This is serious." Her voice sounds excited, too, like Nunzi's.

"You won't believe it," Nunzi says.

I lay out the whole story again for Amber. "It looked just like you. And it sounded like you too."

"Holy crap." Amber looks at Nunzi. He's nodding his head. "Shape shifter."

After a moment Amber says, "You can't go back in there Matty."

"What?!" *That isn't fair!* I want to say. *I made one mistake!*

"Matty," Amber grabs my shoulders and looks me dead in the eye, "A shape shifter is a demon."

10

"Did you see anything else?" Amber is interrogating me inside the van. Black-and-white images from the different cameras glow on screens in front of us. Amber is rewinding and fast forwarding through the video on one of the screens.

"No, I saw you. And then I followed you into the room."

"Did you see that lady you were talking about?"

"LuAnn?"

"Yeah. LuAnn. Did you see her?"

"No. I didn't see anyone once I got inside the room and the door slammed shut."

Amber rests her chin in her left hand as she scans the video. Even though she asked the question, she seems only half-interested in the answer.

"There!" She stops the video and points to the screen. I look at the long hallway in black-and-white, squinting to see whatever she's pointing at. She rewinds and plays again. "See it?" Her finger is still pointing at the screen.

"Uh…" Maybe I should just go along with her, be excited, but I don't see anything.

She rewinds again and points. "There!"

When I don't answer she says, "The door just closed. Watch. Here, you go in, it's open, and now, there! You can see it close."

I keep my eye on the doorway as she rewinds again. I can kind of see something move. "Yeah, I guess I see it." I know I lived it.

"There!" She says again.

"And what happened once you got inside the room? Did you have an EVP going, any equipment with you? Anything?"

"Uh, no." I feel my face blush at this. What kind of ghost hunter am I? "Just my flashlight."

"Well, what happened in there?"

I tell her about seeing her in the room, how it felt like a freezer and I could see my breath, the voices, the cold knob, my flashlight cutting off.

"Jesus," she says.

"I said the spell of protection, prayer, whatever you want to call it," I say quickly. "I said it in my head, anyway."

"Did it help?"

"I think so. Nunzi showed up right after that." Maybe it was just coincidence. I hope not. I hope that spell of protection works. Every. Time.

As the team tears down the electrical workings of ghost hunting, Amber has me stay in the van to help her organize. Lame. I'd rather be doing something more active. As it is, I'm untangling cords and handing them to her.

Kat walks toward me with a tangled cord and hands it to me. "Crazy night, huh?"

"Yeah." She still looks smoking hot. "So," I take a deep breath. "Did you get anywhere?" I nod toward Nunzi.

She looks behind her. "Nah. He's too old for me anyway." She smiles at me and my heart melts.

"Yeah." I take the cord from her and I swear her finger traces along the top of my hand. A flush of heat rises from my toes.

Then she's gone. Back into the convent to get more equipment.

"She's cute," Amber says.

Jesus. Is Amber psychic?

"Yeah, I guess." Now the blush moves to my face.

"I think she likes you."

My heart beats a little harder. Could she? "Nah. I mean, as a friend, yeah, but nothing more. She's straight."

"Uh huh," Amber says with a sly smile.

"No, really, she told me."

"Uh huh." Same smile.

I want to say, "Don't do that. Don't get me thinking, hoping," but I don't say anything. I just try to wipe the smile off my face as I wind the electrical cord onto the spool. Amber keeps working silently in the van.

Before we leave, Amber reminds me to protect myself regularly. "You have to figure out how to hone your gift or you will go crazy, and then you will need that psychiatrist."

"Psychologist," I correct her.

"Psychologist," Amber says with a smile.

"Ready to go?" Kat asks. "It's really late." Then she whispers into my ear, her breath on my earlobe, "My mom would kill me if she knew how late I was getting home tonight." Amber thinks both of our moms know where we're at and wholeheartedly approve in our ghost hunting participation.

Kat told her Mom that she was staying at my house. Unfortunately, I told my mom that I was staying at her house. I'm not sure what we'll do when we get home.

"Hey Kat," Jason calls out. He jogs up to us. "Why don't you guys come crash at my place tonight. Save the drive home for the morning."

Wow. Saved by the cousin. Kat and I agree and follow Jason to his apartment in West Omaha. In the morning, it will only take us a half hour to get back home. Our parents will never be any wiser.

"Sorry I don't have a guest bedroom for you, but this isn't too bad." Jason tugs on the pullout couch. A double-sized bed unfolds before us.

It never occurred to me that Kat and I would have to share a bed. Gulp.

It doesn't seem to faze Kat at all, though. She takes sheets from Jason's arms while I just stand there staring at the bed. Like some zombie lesbian.

"Hey, bright eyes!" Kat says. She throws me one end of the bottom sheet. "Want to help me with this?"

I grab the sheet from her and help her make the bed. That we'll sleep in. Together. I don't have pajamas. She doesn't have pajamas. Oh. My. God. I think fast. I have to keep my wits about me here. I feel more panic now than I did trapped in the room in the convent. "Hey, Jas!" I call out. "Do you have some old t-shirts or something for us to sleep in?"

"Oh yeah, sure." Jason disappears into his bedroom.

Kat is just smiling at me. I feel that blush rise up from my toes and from my chest, both at odds with one another. The one from my toes, excitement. The one from my chest, embarrassment.

Sleep, sleep, sleep. I say in my head like a mantra. *It's just sleep.*

Jason brings two t-shirts back with him, says goodnight, and goes back into his room. *Does he not know I'm a lesbian? Does he not worry that I might compromise his sweet, little cousin?* And before I know it, Jason's sweet, little cousin is peeling her clothes off. Right in front of me! I grab my t-shirt and race to the bathroom. No way am I stripping my clothes in front of her. I don't want her to think I'm after her, even though I am. *Does she know I am?*

Once I'm in the bathroom, I sit on the toilet seat. *Okay, Matty, pull it together. It's just sleeping.* After I calm myself down, I change into the large men's t-shirt that Jason gave us. I slowly open the door and peek around the corner of the hallway out into the living room. Kat is already in bed, under the covers. *Whew.*

I climb into bed next to her and stay on the edge, the farthest away I can get. I don't want her to think I'm after her, which I guess I kind of am, or that I'm going to make a move on her, which I definitely am not.

When I finally settle in with ample space between us Kat says, "Aren't you going to turn out the lights?"

Oh crap. "Oh, yeah." I jump out of my comfy position and go to the light switch at the wall. Once the room is dark, I realize that I'm not afraid of the dark. And I'm not afraid of whatever, or whoever, might show themselves to me. It seems like a first.

"Hello?" Kat's voice slices through the darkness. "Are you coming to bed?"

Gulp. She has a flirty kind of tone to her voice. Now *that* scares me.

I ease into the bed, trying not to disturb the covers, or more importantly, disturb her. I again settle in and leave ample room between me and her. At least I think I do; I'm still at the edge.

"That was ultra-rad." Kat's voice is softer now, almost a whisper.

I'm facing the ceiling with the covers pulled up to my chin. I think she's talking about the ghost hunt. "Yeah, totally." Does she even know what happened to me with the Amber ghost thing and being locked in the room? I don't know. Then I realize that I don't know if anything had happened to *her*. So I ask.

Kat tells me that she and Jason went down to the morgue. She didn't see anything, but while they were doing an EVP session, where they use a dvr to try to record a conversation with spirits, a piece of wood flew out of the darkness and missed Jason's ear by an inch. "He heard it whiz past his ear, that's how close it was," she says.

"Did you get any EVPs?" I ask.

"Not that we heard," Kat turns in the bed. She's facing me now. "Jason said we might hear something when we go through the evidence."

"Yeah." I still have to think of a good excuse to get out of the house so that I can spend five hours in Omaha going through the evidence. Amber said that will start tomorrow at noon. "Pizza first, then evidence scanning," she said.

Then I think, *who am I kidding?* My parents are so busy with that case of Mom's, I can just leave and they won't even know I'm gone. I'll just show up for breakfast, say hey, and go my own way.

I suddenly realize that Kat is talking, but I haven't been listening. She's telling another story about the sanctuary. "...we couldn't figure out where the banging was coming from." Kat ends her story before I have a chance to catch up.

"Oh, uh, that was in the sanctuary, huh?"

"Yeah. Amazing, right?"

"Yeah," I agree because what else can I do? "Amazing."

"Especially given what Amber said about the history of the place."

I totally forgot to ask Amber about that! I turn toward Kat. A small band of light from a streetlight is spilling across Kat's cheek, so I can see nearly her entire face. We're only inches away from each other. My heart pounds in my chest. #ThisGirlisHot.

I catch my breath and say, "What did Amber say?"

Kat is totally oblivious to my shortness of breath and she jumps right into what Amber told her. "The convent was built in the early 1900s. The nuns were Carmelite, whatever that means, and they lived there—"

I chime in, "Oh, they inhabited! Get it? *Inhabited*…habit? Nuns… habit…" Okay, nervous energy has turned into stupidity.

Kat rolls her eyes, then continues, "They lived there until 1989, then they left to start some nursing home in Iowa.

"1989?" I look up into the darkness.

"Yeah."

"And nothing's been there since 1989?"

"I guess not."

"Don't you think that's weird?"

"I don't know. Why?"

Kat's dark eyes blink at me. "The walls, the hallways, everything… they were all so pristine. Even white curtains still hung on all the windows. It's like the nuns left and everything just froze there. I don't even remember seeing dust, do you?"

"Dust?" Kat turns on her back and looks to the ceiling. "Hmmmm." Her nose is perfect. It's the perfect size and has the perfect curve from her eyes to her mouth. "I guess not," she says.

I take my thoughts back to the convent. "I mean, it's just weird. There's no graffiti, no dust, no trash, nothing. It's like the whole building was sealed tight and is just, well, waiting for them all to come back."

"Yeah," Kat says. "Creepy. I never even thought of that."

"Did Amber say anything about a murder or anything? Like, why did that nun with the slashed throat show up?"

"No. She said that there were no newspaper reports, nothing about a murder or anything there. It was totally uneventful."

Now I turn over onto my back again. "Huh." Maybe the nuns

didn't report the murder. Maybe they were protecting someone, or they just didn't want anyone to know. Maybe they covered the whole thing up. Goose bumps run down my spine.

"I guess we'll have to wait to see what the evidence shows," Kat says matter-of-factly.

"I guess so."

"Well, goodnight." Kat suddenly kisses my cheek. Then, she turns over so that her back is to me.

I put my hand over where her kiss left a moist ring. My thoughts race back and forth between the convent and the kiss that just happened. What does Kat think of me? She seems really into Nunzi, but why would she kiss me? Just a kiss between friends, I'm sure. But she knows I'm a lesbian. But she'd kiss a gay guy, too, wouldn't she? And then I think of what Amber said, about Kat liking me and insinuating that she might not be straight after all.

Now I hear Kat softly snore, in an out. Not really a snore, more like a loud breath, kissing the air. *Okay, Matty, get a hold of yourself.*

As I'm listening to her breathing, I suddenly realize that nothing else is going on in the room. There are no visitors, no apparitions begging my attention; no great-grandmother holding onto my feet. All is quiet.

That spell of protection Amber taught me might just work.

I say it one more time before I go to sleep. I drift off wondering what tomorrow will bring. What the evidence from the convent will actually show us.

I try to forget about the awkwardness that took place this morning as Kat and I drive to the warehouse where we're meeting the team for the evidence review. Did I say awkwardness? How about downright embarrassment.

I don't sleep well. I never have. I guess it's because of all the visitors I get throughout the night. At Jason's apartment, I got no visitors. So sleep I did. I never woke up once, at least that I remember. Except...

I obviously woke up enough to take my shirt off in the middle of the night. I guess I was hot or something because I had also thrown the covers off myself. It wasn't until Kat shook me awake that I'd realized what had happened.

Holy crap! And Jason was already up and in the kitchen, rattling around breakfast dishes. So not only did I flash my everything to Kat, but even Jason might have seen! *Oh god.* Of all the nights to sleep so deeply.

Kat laughed it off, as usual. When she woke me up, she just gently pushed on my naked shoulder and whispered, "Hey supermodel, time to get up." I looked at her face, thinking how great it was to see her smile first thing in the morning. I even kind of stretched out. She just kept smiling at me, like the Kat that ate the canary. That's when I realized and quickly pulled the sheet up over myself.

"Oh god, I'm sorry, I—"

"Come on Heidi, Jason's waiting for us in the kitchen." She picked my shirt off the floor and tossed it on top of me.

"Heidi?" I pulled on my shirt and slinked into my jeans.

"Heidi Klum."

I looked at her quizzically for a second then realized she was going back to the supermodel joke. I followed her into the kitchen, wondering if Jason saw me too. Maybe I didn't want to know.

With that embarrassment behind me it was time to focus on the task at hand. I had to come up with an excuse that I wouldn't be home until tonight. Even if Mom hadn't slept at home, she would check in with Sasha about how things were going. I guess technically, Sasha is my "babysitter." Ugh.

Kat came up with a good idea, so I texted my mom and told her that me and Kat were going to hang out and play video games. She texted back to have fun and sent a heart emoji.

"Don't forget to wish your moms 'Happy Mother's Day,'" Jason said.

Oh crap. I texted Mom my Mother's Day message with lots of hug and kiss emojis. #IFG. I feel guilty.

Jason told us that Amber worked for a videographer and she had this warehouse for her work. I didn't even know any videographers lived in Omaha. I was impressed at first, but then we followed Jason into a part of town I'd never been to before. There were graffiti tags everywhere.

We walk through a front office area that's cool and dusty. Then we walk into a huge, empty warehouse. I don't know what videographers do, or why Amber needed to work out of this warehouse, but it's kind of awesome.

The team is set up in a back corner of the warehouse. They sit at a long table with a bunch of monitors and stuff lined up in front of them.

"Hey kids!" Jason's voice echoes off the walls.

"Hey!" the scattered voices echo back. It's Nunzi, Troy, Sara, and Amber. Oh yeah. And LuAnn.

She's sitting there, right next to Amber. Like she belongs with them. Like she's meant to be there. She's looking at me with those steel gray eyes. She doesn't have a kindly smile like old women have; she looks more like a Jessica Lange character in *American Horror Story*.

I turn to Jason, grab his arm, say his name. He turns to me and says, "yeah?" I look back and LuAnn is gone.

I feel cold air rush past me.

"Did you feel that?" I whisper to Kat.

"Huh?"

"Never mind."

Kat and Jason walk toward the table and I quickly follow. I scan the other corners of the room but don't see LuAnn. Then it's suddenly like I'm walking in a tunnel. Everyone is talking to one another, but their voices swirl around me and bounce off the walls that are closing in on me. The light concentrates into small baseball-sized orbs of blue, gold, green, and purple. I'm walking forward with Kat and Jason, but it's like I'm alone. Then Amber grabs my wrist and the whole scene grinds to a halt.

"You okay?" she says and her voice is perfectly normal. The light is normal. I'm back to normal.

At least I think I am.

"Yeah, yeah," I manage to squeak out, but the truth is, I don't know what's happening to me. I feel like I'm kind of losing it.

Nunzi points to the screen in front of him and says something to Amber, which takes her attention away from me for now. I scan the room one more time and take a seat next to Amber. Kat and Jason sit down at the opposite end of the table. Troy and Sara are at another table.

Amber gives me a set of headphones. They're big like Beats, so I feel like I look kind of cool. She tells me that I'll be listening to the EVPs, the digital recordings for any electronic voice phenomena. She points to the screen in front of me and tells me to write down the number that corresponds to what I'm listening to. Then Amber shows me how to go back and start and stop, how to go from one recording to the next. It's all pretty straightforward but I don't want to interrupt her.

"Got it?" she asks.

I nod and start listening. I'm excited at first, excited to be part of the review process and to be part of the team. But then fifteen minutes go by, a half hour, an hour. Nothing. Nothing at all. The only thing I'm listening to are a bunch of questions spoken into the air. I feel like I'm going to fall asleep.

That is, until I get to an EVP; it's with me and Nunzi in the morgue a week ago.

There are the sounds we heard when we listened to it at the van—the gurgling and the lady saying "help," but there were other things, small things, things that make the hair on my arms stand straight up.

Before the gurgling I hear a man's voice. It's very low and almost unintelligible. Like he's mumbling something. I go back and listen to it again. It's almost like Latin or something. I'm not Catholic, don't really know anything about the religion, but it sounds like something from a tv show I saw once. I get an image of a priest walking down the aisle of a Cathedral holding one of those big lanternlike things that incense pours out of. The priest usually waves it back and forth as he walks. And he says something in Latin. It's like that, like this voice is saying Latin in a smooth, almost songlike way.

I listen again. The voice even echoes like in a big room. I can't make out a single word, but I become entranced by it. I almost forget to write down the place where I hear it. I go back again and write down the readings.

I let the audio continue this time and hear the gurgling. I hear Nunzi yell and the flashlight fall. I hear footsteps and then I can hear the man say it very clearly. His voice growls this time.

My hands shake as I go back to the spot on the recording. I hold the Beats-style headphones close to my ears. There's no mistaking it.

I hear Nunzi pounding on the door and the sound of both of us breathing heavily. Then I hear the woman say "heeeeelp" again and in the background, barely audible, the man's voice moaning. I go back and listen again. I write down the exact spot I hear the moan.

I pull off the headphones and look at Amber. I guess my face gives me away or something because she immediately pulls off her headphones and says, "What's wrong?"

"I found something."

"Are you okay? Maybe you need some water or something? You look pale and you're covered in sweat."

I swallow down the dryness in my throat and nod to her. As she gets a bottle of water for me, I wipe the sweat off my face.

"What'd you find?" Amber asks as she hands me the bottle.

My hands are still shaking and I try to make them stop, but the more I try, the more they shake.

"What is it Matty?" Amber's voice is more urgent this time.

"Well, maybe you should listen…" I don't know what else to say.

Amber plugs her earphones into the amp so I put on my headphones and find the location on the recording. Exactly to where it sounds like a priest chanting. I feel a sense of pride at marking the spot right. I look at Amber as she listens. The woman gurgles, she says "help." The flashlight drops, footsteps, I look at the needle on the indication and look at my page. It's almost here.

I put my finger up when the man is about to say it, then point at Amber as his voice peals, "Matilda Patterson."

Amber's mouth falls open and she pulls the headphones off. I do the same. "What?!?" She says it so loud that everyone else stops what they're reviewing and look at us. Amber says, "Oh you guys, you have to hear this!"

She unplugs both sets of headphones and turns the speakers toward the other end of the table. Troy and Sara gather in behind us. "Go back to the chanting," she instructs me.

I rewind the track to the exact spot and hit play.

It all plays again and Nunzi looks about as white as I did when I heard it. "Crap," he whispers.

Amber shuts off the recording after the man says my name. "There's more," I say. I tap the play button again and there's the woman saying "heeeeelp" then the man moaning. It makes the hair on my arms rise once again.

Everyone listens one more time, then Amber taps off the recording. "Well, we know it's not residual," Amber says, then she looks at me. "How are you doing?"

"Uh…okay…I guess." But I'm not okay. That man-ghost said my name. My whole name. I mean, it wasn't like he was just repeating after Nunzi. Nunzi never called me Matilda Patterson in that morgue. "How…how did he know…"

"Your name?" Amber finishes my sentence.

"Yeah."

"Hard to say. Could have been LuAnn again."

"But this was a man…"

"If she's a shape-shifter like we think she is, she can be whoever suits her—man, woman, child, dog. Whatever."

"Why is she after me anyway? What does she want from me?"

"Hmmm." Amber thinks about this for a moment. I look down the table and everyone is listening to us, watching us. They seem as on the edge of their seats as I am. Even Kat looks a bit more concerned than she has so far.

And then I manage to say it. "I saw her when we walked in here."

"In here?" Amber repeats. "Today?"

"Yeah. She was sitting right next to you when we came in."

"Oh," Amber sits back in her chair. "That's why you looked white as a ghost this morning."

"Did I?"

"And you were kind of in a trance."

I just nod. I guess that's what it felt like too.

Amber turns her chair toward me and grabs my hands. "Matty, it could be that she doesn't want something from you. It could be that it's you she wants."

"Me? What do you mean me?"

"It could be that LuAnn is trying to take you over. She sees you as a vulnerable, easy target."

I sit up straight and pull my hands from Amber's grip. "I'm not weak."

"No, no—I don't mean it that way. But you can see her, you can hear her, you can feel her presence. In fact, she might see you as very strong, and she wants to take you over so that together, you are a destructive force."

"You keep saying 'take me over'—what do you mean? Like get inside of me?"

"Exactly. She wants to take over your body to wreak some havoc in our world."

I swallow hard. Everyone is still looking at me. Kat's brow is furrowed in concern.

"But I don't want that. I don't want any of this! Make her stop!"

"Did you say your protection spell this morning?"

"No, I forgot." I feel a line of red rise up from my neck into my face as I think of my exposed nakedness with Kat this morning.

"Say it now," Amber says, and she is completely serious. And urging.

"Right here?" I look down the row again. Jason and Troy put their headphones on and turn back to their screens as if to give me privacy, but Nunzi, Sara, and Kat are still looking at me.

Amber calls over her shoulder, "Back to work everyone." Then she turns back to me. "Say. It. Now." It's a command, not a request. "Here, I'll say it with you." She again grabs both of my hands and together, we recite the spell of protection she taught me.

"Now, it's really important for you to say this every morning and every night. It wouldn't hurt to say it during the day either, and definitely anytime you feel like LuAnn is close by."

"But maybe I won't know she's close by—I mean, if she can become anyone and anything."

"You need to use your sixth sense. If anything feels amiss, trust your instinct. Besides, it won't hurt to say the spell from time to time."

"Yeah." But with all the ghosts I see, I could be doing this fifty times a day!"

Amber grabs my chin in her hand and looks directly into my eyes. "Promise me."

"Yes," I say stronger, "I promise."

After I say the spell of protection, I kind of relax. It's really freaky having a ghost say your name, especially if they're a killer. But Amber thinks the voice is from that crazy LuAnn trying to get inside my head.

When everyone takes a break from watching video screens and listening intently to EVPs, I take the opportunity to talk to Amber about the history of the convent. Besides, Kat seems quite engaged in conversation with Nunzi and talking to Amber is a good way to distract myself.

Amber tells me that she went to the public library, the Omaha Historical Society, and even to the diocese to find out about the abandoned building. It was built in 1925 by the Catholic Church and served as a convent for sixty-some years.

"The Catholic Church sold it to a developer in 1990, but the developer never did anything with it," Amber says.

"Why not?"

"I've left messages for the developer to ask that very question, but he hasn't returned my calls. He's some guy who flips houses and is really into theatre. He owns the small theatre in Dundee—the one where they do plays. Do you know the one?"

I shake my head no.

"Well, this is the biggest property he's ever bought."

"What's his name?" Like I'm going to know who he is, but something compels me to ask.

"John Abernath. Why?"

I shrug. "I don't know." But I grab a pen and paper from the table and write his name down.

"Do you want his number too?" Amber is being sarcastic but I say yes. She gives me the number and watches me write it down.

"What are you going to do?"

"I don't know," I repeat.

Amber looks at me for a second. "I don't know if I trust you with that number, Matty. I don't even know why I gave it to you. But if you call him, you have to be professional."

"I don't know that I'll *call* him." I stare down at the numbers. I feel like I'm not even the one talking. I don't know who's talking right now. LuAnn? "I just feel like I need to know."

"Know what?"

"What happened there. Why he hasn't torn it down."

"Just remember, he was nice enough to let us into the property."

"Have you met him?"

"Only his assistant. She's the one who met us there to give us the keys and she's the one I'll give the keys back to."

"What's her name?" I have my pen at the ready. Who am I?

"Really, Matty?"

I look Amber dead in the eye. "What's her name?"

"Jill something or other. I don't know."

I keep looking Amber in the eye.

"Jill Blake."

I write down the name. Now I'm starting to wonder who's helping Amber talk. It's like we're acting out a play or something. We're the actors, but someone else has written the script.

Amber is staring at me, but not like she's mad or anything, more like she's in a trance.

"I don't know why I asked all of that," I say blankly.

Amber blinks. "I don't know why I told you."

I fold the piece of paper and throw it on the table. "I won't do anything, I promise."

Amber takes a deep breath. "That was weird."

"Right?" I'm glad she felt it too.

"So, did you find out anything about a murdered nun?"

"What?" Amber seems distracted by what just happened. She kind of shakes her head and lets out an exhale, then says "no."

"Really?" I'm shocked.

Now she's back to normal Amber. "I checked the newspapers, the historical society, I even asked the diocese—and believe me, they didn't like the question—and there was nothing."

"Why would the diocese have a problem with that question?"

"You don't know much about the Catholic church, do you?"

I shrug.

"Well, talking about murder or scandal within the church is not their forte."

"Do you think they're hiding something?"

"Hard to tell. I mean, they just don't like to talk about such things."

"What's a diocese anyway?" I feel stupid, but I really don't understand.

"It's like the headquarters of the church for Omaha and a few suburbs."

"Where are they?"

"Oh no," Amber wags her finger at me and walks away.

"What was that about?" Kat startles me as she walks up behind me. "Wow. Jumpy much?"

"Nothing. I guess maybe I was too pushy."

"I was thinking about that voice knowing your name."

"Yeah?"

"Mrs. P calls you Matilda."

"Yeah, so?"

"So, that guy that showed up in English Lit. What if he's the one at the convent?"

"Why would he be?"

"I don't know, but maybe he has something to do with all of this."

I'd never considered that. Can a ghost be there and then be here? I guess, why not? But why would he show up at school and then follow me here? I don't get very far into my pondering because Kat quickly informs me that the guys want to go out for a burger and they want us to join them. *Oh great.* Here we go. Kat is just like the other girls at school. I feel my stomach tighten. "You really like him, don't you?" I don't like the tone of my voice, but it just came out.

"Oh, come on," Kat nudges my shoulder, "jealous much?"

I feel a rush of blood rise from my chest into my face. I don't know how to respond, so I say "Whatever," and walk away.

Kat gives a little laugh behind me, which kind of pisses me off. I see Nunzi and Troy sitting at the table behind a monitor. They look up when they hear Kat call out to me, "So can we go?" All eyes seem to be on me.

Well, what can I do now? "Sure. We can go." I sound less than enthusiastic. Then, without thinking, I say, "Hey Amber, you want to come too?" I don't know why she'd want to hang out with a bunch of kids. Well, it's not like she's *that* old, but still…

Amber looks at Nunzi and Troy, then back at me. Then she says, "Yeah, I'll come too. Why not?"

Kat bumps me as she passes me and heads back to the table. She whispers, "Inviting the boss? Thanks a lot."

"Jason, Sara, you want to come too?" I shout across the room. We might as well be one, big happy family.

"I've got a family thing, otherwise I would go," Sara says.

"Jason?" I yell in his direction.

He pulls one side of his earphones off. "What?"

"We're going out for burgers after this," Amber says. "Chaperones." She winks at Jason.

He smiles wickedly and says, "Oh yeah, sounds great."

Kat turns and looks at me, exasperated.

I just give her a little smile, then get back to investigating.

The burger place is not very busy when we get there, so finding a table for all of us is no problem. We go up and place our orders in threes. Kat goes up with Nunzi and Troy. "So which one do you think she likes?" Jason asks, more out of concern than gossip.

"I don't know." I shrug.

Amber gives me a sympathetic look. Like she knows. I feel heat rise into my face.

"Maybe I should just have a talk with both of them," Jason says.

Talk? What's he going to say?

"They're both too old for her."

For a minute, I feel hope rise in my chest, but then I think Amber will probably tell him to back off; that he's being too protective. But that's not what she says at all.

"I think that's a good idea," Amber says. She looks over my shoulders to the counter where the trio is. "She's looking for affirmation, you know."

Jason and I both look at Amber quizzically.

"She just wants to know that someone finds her attractive."

Someone! I think. *I'm someone.*

As if Amber can hear my thoughts, she says, "Boys, that is. She wants to know if boys find her attractive."

There comes the heat rising up my neck and into my face. I look down at my cell.

"Yeah, well…" Jason says. He's turned around in his chair, watching the trio goofing around and Kat annoyingly giggling.

They come back to the table and now Amber, Jason, and I need to go to the counter to place our orders. Jason glares at Nunzi and Troy as he stands up, but they're oblivious. Kat is holding court, after all. Seriously, it's like Nunzi and Troy are hanging onto every word she says. Ugh!

It makes me so nauseated that I consider ordering a salad! But, instead I order cheese frenchies and onion rings. This place is famous for their cheese frenchies—basically a grilled cheese sandwich that's breaded and deep fried. Yummy goodness. Add a strawberry shake and I have successfully ordered a million-calorie meal that will harden my arteries well into adulthood.

As I carry my tray of deep-fried yumminess back to the table I see Nunzi feed Kat a French fry. I glance over at Jason, but he's still at the counter with his back to this awful scene. Kat laughs while she wipes some ketchup from her lip.

Oh brother.

I sit down next to Troy and I can feel myself glaring at Kat and Nunzi, even though I'm trying not to. I look down at my stacked deep-fried Frenchie and have really lost my appetite.

A tray drops down on the table and I jump about a foot off my chair.

Jason is standing at the end of the table and now he's glaring at Nunzi.

"Rule number-one." Jason's voice is strong, firm. "No dating ANYONE on the team."

Nunzi kind of shrinks away from Kat.

"Rule number-two." Jason continues. "This one is a life rule, not a team rule." He leans over the table toward Nunzi, then glances over at Troy, as if to include him. "No dating a girl under the age of 18. You know what they call that?" He's glaring at Nunzi again.

Nunzi's Adams apple rises, seems to get stuck for a minute, then drops back down.

Jason picks up his tray, walks behind Nunzi, then motions for Nunzi to move over.

Nunzi reluctantly complies and Jason sits down between Kat and Nunzi.

"Nothing was happening..." Kat whines.

Jason cuts her off, "Don't want to hear it."

I try to hide the smile that wants to creep onto my face, so I take a long sip of my strawberry shake. I feel happy. Really happy. Shamefully happy.

That is, until I think back on rule number-one: No dating anyone on the team. I guess that goes for me and Kat too.

Amber and Jason said that we'd be back at the convent at the beginning of June for another round of ghost hunting.

That worked out for me because I had to focus my energy on finals, the prom I never went to, and saying a lot of words of protection. It seemed to help.

But today is the first day of summer break and there's nothing to do now but sit with my thoughts, and my dreams.

The nun has visited me there.

In last night's dream, she was whole; there was no slash across the throat or gasping for air. She was young. Younger than I thought. Like maybe twenty, or a teenager, or something. She was walking across a courtyard carrying something beneath her whipple. At least I think that's what they call that black robe-like thing that nuns wear. Flowers were blooming all around her, but she was carrying that something so close to her it looked like she was cold and pulling it into herself to stay warm.

She opened the door to the chapel, looked around, and ducked inside.

Another nun crossed the courtyard. She had something in her hand, but I couldn't see what it was because she was trying to hide it. When she got to the chapel door, she pressed her ear against the door for a minute, then looked around and entered.

Suddenly I was in the middle of the empty courtyard, so I stepped closer and closer to the door. Singing came from inside the chapel. Two voices. No, not singing, yelling.

Then something grabbed my ankles.

I woke up with a start. My great-grandma, at least the spirit that looked like my great-grandma was at the foot of my bed, holding onto my ankles, and staring at me. She was glowing in the dark and I could see right through her. She was old, like the picture Mom has. She was wearing a housecoat. We looked at each other for a minute, then she shook her head no, and then she just disappeared.

I woke up around 9:00. And now I'm staring at the piece of paper with John Abernath's name and phone number written on it.

Here's the creepy thing: I had crumpled up this piece of paper a few weeks ago and had thrown it away in the trash can in my room.

This morning, it was on my wobbly desk, pressed out for me to see again. So now I'm holding that creased-up little paper in my hand when my cell phone rings. Kat. I take a deep breath. "Hello?"

"Whatchya doin?" Kat has a way of sounding flirty no matter what she says. It doesn't really go with her image, but that's Kat.

"Nothing." Mom and Dad are at work. Sasha is doing Sasha things. Just sitting around."

"Wanna go to Omaha?"

I look at the paper in my hand. "Um...to do what?"

"I don't know, go to the mall. It's better than sitting around here."

I look at the clock. It's not even 9:30. Mom and Dad won't be home for another six or seven hours, at least.

"Yeah. Sure. But I need to shower and eat something." I crumple up the piece of paper and again throw it in my trash can. "Maybe we can stop at Burger King on the way out of town?"

"You'll pick me up then?"

"Yeah. See you in, like, an hour."

A quick shower and then I'm out. I get my clothes together and leave them on the bed as I go take a shower. When I come back with a towel draped around me, I see something on top of my clothes.

"John Abernath." The piece of paper I threw in the trash can. Right on top of my clothes, the little piece of paper where I have the name and number of the guy who owns the convent. The paper is wrinkled but flattened.

"Crap," I whisper, and I look around the room to make sure I'm alone. I quickly throw on my clothes, stuff the little piece of paper in my back pocket and head out the door.

Kat has her feet up against the glovebox with her knees scrunched up closer to her as she paints fresh polish on her fingernails. I don't know how she does that in a moving car, but she does.

I have the back windows rolled down, and the front ones down a crack and the wind is swirling around in the car with such velocity that even my short hair is being whipped out of place. But I like it. I like how it feels on the open road.

About halfway to Omaha, I finally tell her about the piece of paper that refused to be thrown away.

"For real?" she drops her feet to the floor of the car.

I nod my head.

"Let's do it!" She grabs her cell phone and waggles her black fingernails at me as if to say *gimme the number*. I point to the glovebox.

There's part of me that thinks we shouldn't do this. But there's another part that can't stand not knowing more about that place and why it's still standing there like a forgotten monument.

Kat starts punching in numbers.

"Wait!" I grab her wrist. I swear I can feel her pulse against my fingertip. My heart flutters and I let go. Quickly. "I mean... I promised Amber that I wouldn't call it."

I glance over just enough to see Kat give me a wide grin. "Yeah, but you're not calling the number. I am." Her fingers start tapping again and I hear it ringing.

"Wait!!" I yell loud enough to make Kat quickly hang up.

"What?!?"

"What are you... we... going to say?" I mean, we can't just call and wing it. We need to have some credibility.

"Good point." Kat rests back into the seat and looks out onto the road ahead of us.

I grip the steering wheel so hard my fingertips are turning white. My heart is beating a mile a minute.

"I've got it!" Kat says and starts tapping her phone screen. Before I gulp down the dryness in my throat to tell her to stop, a woman's voice comes through the speakerphone.

"John Abernath's office, Victoria speaking."

Gulp.

"Hello Victoria, is John available?"

"May I tell him who's calling?"

Kat looks at me slyly, like she's totally fearless.

"This is his daughter."

His daughter! Is she nuts?

"Oh, hi Suze! Just a minute and I'll connect you."

"Holy...!" I yell. I can't believe that worked!

Kat smiles at me in a way that makes my toes tingle.

"Crap, crap, crap!!" I grip the wheel even harder.

"Hi sweetie." A deep, soft voice comes out of the speakerphone.

I swallow hard.

"Actually, my name is Kat and I wanted to talk to you about your convent."

"Excuse me?" The voice is not so soft now and I think it raised an octave.

"I was part of the team that investigated there recently."

"I don't know who you are, young lady, but I'm going to hang up now."

Well, at least he's polite.

Kat talks quickly, "I want to talk to you about the nun with the slit throat."

Silence.

Dead silence.

I think he may have hung up.

"Go on," he says.

Crap, crap, crap!!

Kat shoves the phone in front of my mouth. "Go on," she whispers.

I'm going to kill her!

"Uh..."

"Young lady?" He sounds like he's losing his patience—quickly.

"My name is Matty and I was part of the ghost hunting team that was in your convent." Maybe I shouldn't have said that; Amber's going to kill me.

He doesn't respond. Again, there's just silence.

"Hello?" I ask.

"I'm listening."

"Why haven't you done anything with the property?"

He doesn't say anything for a moment, then he says, "You said something about a nun."

"Yes."

"That's why."

"Because of the nun?"

"Yes."

"Do you know something about her?"

"Do you?"

Okay. Now I feel like I'm talking to my little brother, if I had a little brother. I wish I had time to think this through. I glare at Kat, thinking of how mad I am that she even called the number.

"Can I come talk to you in person?"

There's a pause again, then, "Do you know where my office is?"

"Uh...no."

"Regency Court." Kat starts tapping into her phone while he gives the address.

"I'll be there in 45 minutes."

"I'll see you then." He says it in such a way that I wonder if his assistant will send us packing once we show up. I guess time will tell.

The offices of J. Abernath and Company are like out of a movie. There's a curved reception desk with frosted glass at the front and rich wood on the top held in place with stainless steel rods. #swanky

There's a woman in her twenties sitting at the reception desk with a headset.

"Can I help you?" The girl raises the microphone of the headset above her forehead.

Kat and I are not dressed for this at all. We're wearing shorts. Kat nudges me.

"Oh...uh...I'm here for Mr. Abernath. I mean, I have an appointment, sort of." I don't really know how to talk to a receptionist. I'm just going by what I've seen in movies.

"Can I tell him who's here?" She looks from me to Kat and back to me, waiting for an answer.

"I'm...well..." Amber told us to be discreet when we talked about a job. Very discreet. She said some people were embarrassed about having their property searched for ghosts.

Kat nudges me again and then says, "We called him about an hour ago and talked to him about one of his properties. My name's Matty; he's expecting us."

The woman looks at us suspiciously. "And he said he'd meet with you? Now?"

Kat gives a definitive yes.

The woman dials in some numbers, then says, "Jill, there are a couple of girls here to see Mr. Abernath. They say they have an appointment."

The woman listens for a minute, then says to us, "Go to the end of that hallway and turn left, you'll see a desk. That's Jill. She'll take you from there."

Geez. Where are we going? Into some kind of labyrinth?

We approach a woman my mom's age: old. She's wearing glasses and a nice dress with a cardigan. She's actually kind of pretty for someone nearly forty.

"Are you Jill?" Kat asks.

"Yes, and you're meeting Mr. Abernath about the property?"

Kat and I look at each other. "Uh," I say in my most professional voice, "property? Like, the convent? That's what we're here about."

Jill motions for me to keep my voice down, then leans in and whispers, "Yes, the *property*."

I look around and see no one in sight, but if it makes Jill feel better... I guess they're keeping the convent on the DL.

Jill stands up and motions us to follow her. We go down another long hallway with some cool, modern lights hitting blank, gray walls. Jill knocks on the door at the end of the hallway. "Mr. Abernath?" She pokes her head around the door but keeps her body outside with us. Some mumbled words are exchanged behind the door, then she opens it and motions for us to go in.

John Abernath is younger than I expected. I thought he'd be, like, really old. But he's just a little bit older than my dad. He's dressed in a blue button-down shirt and nice jeans. He looks kind of like Jake Gyllenhaal, but not quite. His eyes are a bit beady rather than brooding.

He motions for us to sit as he leans back on his desk like a teacher. "You're both much younger than I thought."

"Same to you," Kat says.

"You were at my property?"

Here we go with the "property" thing again. "Yes," I say, "we were part of the ghost hunting team."

"You're a bit young to be ghost hunting, aren't you? What are you? Fifteen, sixteen?"

"Um...seventeen?" My voice goes up so it sounds like I'm questioning my own answer.

"Seventeen," he repeats as he looks back and forth between us, but not in a creepy way. Still more in a teacher way. "Still a bit young to be doing that kind of work."

"She's a medium," Kat says like it's no big thing.

"Well, not a medium," I glare at Kat. "I just... I can... I..."

"Sense things?" Mr. Abernath asks.

"Well, yeah, I guess."

He extends his hand and says, "I'm John."

I shake his hand and say, "I'm Matty, and this is Kat."

"So, you mentioned the nun."

The nun. Not a nun, or some nun. The nun.

"Um, yeah," I say clumsily, "do you know anything about her?" Oh crap. Crappy crap crap crap. Why did I let Kat talk me into this? I sound anything but professional.

"What do you know about her?"

I look up at Mr. Abernath, leaning back on his desk, and I feel like I'm in the principal's office. Not that I've ever been in the principal's office...

"She saw her," Kat blurts out.

I feel a blush rise from my toes all the way up to my face. Part of me wants to kill Kat for just saying it out loud like that, but the other part of me wonders why we're all being so secretive.

"You...saw her?"

I look down at my feet. I want to run out of here, run to my car, jump in, turn on the ignition, and go. Go as fast as I can away from here.

Suddenly, Mr. Abernath is bending down in front of me, his hand on top of my hand. I'm glad he doesn't have a creepy vibe, otherwise this would feel totally creepy. "Tell me," he says softly, "tell me what you saw."

I look up into his eyes and feel like I'm going to cry. I don't even know why. I swallow hard. I nod my head and say, "Can I have a drink of water?"

He stands up and says, "Sure, sure." He walks over to a sink area he has in his office and opens a cabinet. There's a mini fridge there. The guy has a mini fridge in his office!

He hands me the bottle of water and I drink nearly half the bottle. I only stop because I start to get brain freeze.

He pulls up a chair next to me and leans down so that his elbows rest on his knees.

"Well..." I start, then look at Kat. How did it come to this? I was here to get information, not give it. Then I tell him the story about seeing the nun in the morgue, but I leave out her slit throat.

John leans back in his chair. I think he looks kind of pale, but I'm not sure.

"So..." I try to snap him out of wherever his thoughts have taken him. "Do you know anything about her? Or the convent? Or anything?"

"What did she look like?"

"Well... a... a nun. I mean, she had on that habit thing or whatever, only without the head covering part, and she was young."

He quickly stands up and goes behind his desk. He digs an

iPad out of the drawer and starts tapping on the screen. It takes so long I think he may have forgotten us or something.

"We were hoping to find out why you haven't done something with the convent." Now I'm the one blurting things out, but this guy seems to have lost his grip on the present somehow.

My statement/question doesn't faze him. He's still tapping crazily on his iPad screen.

"Here!" he says and turns the screen around. "Is that her?"

A black-and-white image of a teenage girl is on the screen. She's about my age.

"Uh..." I try to see something in her face that brings me back to the nun at the convent. "I didn't really look at her face that closely. I mean, I saw her face for a second..." My mind drifts off to the horrible slash across her throat, her windpipe being exposed. It kind of took my attention away from her face.

John looks disappointed. He turns the iPad around and looks down at the screen. "Yeah," he says. "I mean with her throat and all, what else can you see?"

Weird. "Kat, we'd better get going." I look at my watch and stand up.

Kat looks at me, stunned. "Huh?"

"We're going to be late." I wiggle my fingers in her direction as if to say come on, let's go.

"Late...?"

"For coffee with Jason."

Kat looks from me to John. We're not having coffee with Jason and I can tell she's trying to figure out what's going on. "Uh, yeah." She stands up slowly.

"It was nice to meet you, Mr. Abernath." I turn and go toward the door.

"Why don't you do something with the place?" Kat gets right to the point.

I turn abruptly, "Kat..."

"I wondered when you might ask," Mr. Abernath smiles at me in a way that makes chills run up my back. "Maybe you should ask your friend," he says.

Kat looks toward me, her eyes wide.

"Ms. Patterson?" John splays his hand out toward a chair, motioning for me to take a seat.

I don't sit. My mind is reeling, I can't even take in all that I think I know, but then it just comes out. I look from Kat to John and say, "Because the nun..."

John leans back on his desk. Kat stands still, staring at me.

"...is your sister."

"She wasn't a nun, you know."

We're standing on the stairs in front of the convent. The heavy wooden doors looming in front of us. John fiddles with a ring of keys to find the one that will open the giant doors.

"Then why was she dressed like one?" Kat is totally unconcerned that we're here without the team. All I can think is that Amber is going to kill me.

"She was in Witness Protection."

Witness Protection? Like in Sister Act? That's what I think, but I don't say it out loud.

"Like in *Sister Act*?" Leave it to Kat to say it out loud.

"She saw something." John finds the key and the big door creaks as it opens into the round, cavernous room. There's a little bit of sunlight streaming in through windows at the top of the entrance. This is the room where the confessionals are.

"Something...?" Kat tries to lead him into saying more, but he completely ignores her.

"A drug deal. A big one. Involved the Feds. I bought this place because I didn't want someone else tearing it down." His voice echoes as he looks around the room. "She's my sister, and I feel like she's here."

"Have you ever seen her?" Kat asks.

"Once. That's how I know about..." he pauses and looks at me. I see his Adam's apple bounce up and down, like he's swallowing hard. He doesn't have to say it; I know he means her throat. He saw her slashed throat.

"How did you know she was here?" I ask. "I mean before you bought the place."

"We knew she was here. Then she wasn't. But her body was never found. All they found was blood. A lot of blood."

He walks toward the door that leads to the sanctuary. "Then, I started to hear that this place was haunted. The nuns taught at the school across the street. They told the kids stories."

He leads us into the big sanctuary where the statue of Jesus nailed to the cross hangs behind the pulpit. More sunlight fills this room and it streams in through plain glass windows that line up on both sides. Some of the pews are still in place as if waiting for a sermon after all these years. "All of the blood was up there." He turns around and points up to the dark, wooden-railed balcony.

Kat and I both look in the direction he's pointing.

"Do you know what happened?" Kat's voice is soft and shaky.

John's footsteps echo around us as he walks toward the statue of Jesus. It seems like maybe he's saying a prayer or something. Kat and I look at each other, not knowing what to do. Oh, how I wish Amber was here. She'd know the questions to ask, what to say.

"You saw her?" John is gazing up at the statue of Jesus.

"Yes," I say. "In the morgue and upstairs in one of the rooms."

He turns around. "The morgue?"

I shake my head as his eyes twinkle with what I think are tears. "Yeah. Downstairs."

"Let's go down there." He grabs my arm and starts pulling me toward the long hallway.

"I don't think this is such a good idea," Kat has real fear in her voice now. I want to say, *you're the one who got us into this mess.* But I don't. I don't want John to think that I think this is a mess. It is...was... his sister, after all.

"I want to see her," John sounds resolute.

"I don't think she's there," I say, even though I'm not really sure. "I mean, I think she was only there to get my attention. She knew..."

John moves in front of me. At first, I think he's mad or something, the way he inches toward me, towering. I try to swallow, but my throat is so dry I feel like I might choke. Then he says, "She knew you could see her, sense her."

I nod my head, "Yeah, I guess." I really need some water.

"Take me to her," he commands.

"I... it doesn't...I mean..." I've never wished more than I have in this moment that I could see a spirit, especially one who's throat is slit.

He grabs my arm, hard. "Take. Me. To. Her." His eyes have changed somehow. I feel myself trembling.

"Hey, look, John..." Kat grabs his wrist and tries to pull him off me. "Let's calm down here for a second."

John lets go of me and starts to cry. I've never seen a grown man cry before. I look at Kat, then take a step back.

John drops into a pew, his head in his hands, his cries echoing off the walls of the chapel.

"What were you two thinking?!?" Amber is pacing back and forth in the same warehouse where we reviewed footage, and Jason is looking agitated as well. We called Jason right away after we got back to my car. John had escorted us out of the convent, then he'd quietly walked back to his car and drove off. Jason told us to meet him at the warehouse, and Amber evidently wanted to rip into us too.

I glare at Kat, who is picking at excess fingernail polish on her left hand, pretending she doesn't care that we're getting reamed, but I know she cares.

"We just wanted to find out more—" I hear a little bit of a whine in my voice and I try to control it. I try to sound more adult-like.

"Find out more!?! I told you guys that he didn't want to talk about this. I can't believe you did this!"

Wow. If I'd known Amber would get this mad—

"This is unbelievable." Amber tugs on Jason's sleeve and they walk over to a table where Amber is rifling through some folders.

Kat finally looks up from her fingernails, glances my way, and shrugs.

Amber is moving her arms around while she's talking to Jason. I don't know if we should just leave, or maybe she's not done with us yet.

When she walks toward us again with a folder in her hand and Jason right beside her, I know she's not done with us yet.

"Okay. Here's the deal. If you're going to be on our team, then you need to stick to your jobs. Your jobs are to support us on ghost hunting missions. Period. You're not supposed to go digging deeper unless we tell you to. Got it?"

"We both mumble a 'yes.'"

"Hey. Look at me," Amber's voice is so firm, how can we not? But I'd rather crawl into a hole right now. "Got it?"

"Yes." We both say simultaneously, with a bit more force this time.

"Now," her voice softens. "Take a seat over at the table."

We do as she tells us to and she and Jason sit down directly across from us.

She takes a deep sigh, then shoves the folder toward us.

"What's this?" I ask.

"Open it. Read it."

I open the folder and Kat looks over my shoulder. I can't believe it. I look up at Amber, who nods her head. I move the folder toward Kat so she can see it too.

I can hear Kat gulp and then she says, "Holy crap."

Brother Arrested in Murder of Omaha Woman. That's the headline glaring off the page at us.

"Uh..." It's all I can think to say. My mind is blank.

"Go ahead. Read the story."

My mind goes all over the place as I read. Summary? John was arrested in the murder of his sister.

"But...how can this be?" I manage to squeak out.

"He seemed like such a nice guy..." Kat says. "A little dramatic, but—"

"He was never convicted, so we shouldn't play jury, but still, you guys are in way over your heads," Amber still sounds mad. And I guess I can kinda see why.

"So now what do we do?" I ask.

"Tell me what happened. From the beginning. And don't leave anything out, even if you think it will get you in trouble." Amber sounds like the big sister I always wanted instead of the stupid one I have.

"It was all Matty's idea," Kat accuses.

"Hey—"

"Never mind all that," Amber says. "Just tell me what happened."

I launch into the story about how we went to John's office and told him about the nun with the slashed throat. And then how we ended up driving over to the convent—which was his idea—and then how he broke down, right there in the chapel.

"Did he say anything?"

"No, he was just crying," I say.

"Yeah, like bad," says Kat. "It was kinda uncomfortable."

"No lie," I say.

Amber's eyes follow us back and forth like she's watching a tennis match. Then she grabs my hands as if to pull my attention back to the task at hand. "Then what?"

"Well, he...he... kinda let out this howling cry..." I say, trying best to describe it.

"Yeah, like a wolf or something. He even had spit flying out of his mouth." Kat paints a pretty good image. It was like he was breaking out of his skin, wanting to rip his shirt off. Like he was becoming a werewolf or something.

"Matty?" Amber takes me out of the image, begging me to say more.

"Then he stood and demanded that I take him to his sister. He was like, crying all over me."

"It was freaky," says Kat.

"Yeah, freaky scary."

"And then what?!?" Amber demands.

"I did it. I took him to his sister."

"What do you mean?" Amber releases her grip on my wrists. Shock washes over her face.

"We went down to the mortuary. He... well, he..."

"Shoved her there," Kat says without hesitation. "He was mad. Real mad."

Amber looks back at me. "He physically shoved you?!"

I rolled up the sleeve of my shirt. There are bruises where his fingers dug into my flesh.

"Oh, that's it! We're calling the police." Amber pulls her cell phone out of her back pocket and starts tapping the screen.

"Wait! It wasn't him!" I say quickly.

"What do you mean? Was he was possessed?!?" There's sarcasm in her tone.

"I don't know, maybe, but what I mean is that he didn't kill her."

Amber rattled the paper with the big headline. "And how do you know?!?"

"Because... well, because..." Kat gives me a little shoulder bump. "Because she told me."

I feel like I'm going to cry. I just want to go home. Why can't they all leave me alone?

"Okay," Amber sounds stern. "You two need to tell me the whole truth, right now."

"We went to the mortuary. John was really upset; crying and groaning. Once he got to the mortuary, he yelled at me that I needed to call his sister right then. But there was nothing there. I could feel it the minute we stepped into the mortuary. It was just cold and dark and empty."

"John had that death grip on Matty's arm," Kat says. "And he kept shaking her and yelling at her to get his sister for him. I told him it didn't work like that. I told him Matty couldn't just will a spirit to talk to her. They had to want to talk to her."

"He didn't like that," I say. "So Kat said that we should go back to the sanctuary. Back to where she was murdered; that maybe I could talk to her there."

"Yeah, that John, he was desperate."

"He wasn't convinced at first, but I told him that we needed to calm down and get in the right frame of mind. That I couldn't talk to anyone unless I was able to focus on what was around me instead of the pain on my arm."

"I just told him, 'come on, John, let's go upstairs and let Matty do her thing.'"

I can see the image in my head as we relay the story to Amber and Jason. We finally got John calmed down enough that he was willing to move upstairs, and to release the death grip on my arm.

We moved to the balcony in the sanctuary and stood at the spot where John said they found a lot of blood. He looked at me with desperation and said, "talk." I glanced at Kat who had a look of desperation in her eyes, too, but it was a the fearful kind.

I closed my eyes and took a deep breath. Like I told John in the sanctuary, spirits have to want me to see them; I can't just tune them in like a tv show. Just like in the sanctuary I felt no presence there. The air was just the air; it hadn't changed; the energy hadn't shifted. I opened my eyes to see John and Kat glaring at me with those pleading looks.

"She says she's sorry she left." I don't know where that came from, but I was feeling desperate myself. Desperate enough to start making stuff up.

John gasped, then started crying again. "I knew it. I knew she didn't want to leave," he said quietly, with his head down.

Kat's eyes were begging me to continue.

"Uh... she wants you to know that she loves you." I knew it was wrong to be making this all up, but I was starting to feel like Kat and I were in danger.

Again, John just sobbed.

"And she wants you to continue living your life. She's fine." I just thought of the most common things spirits always want loved ones to know. "Oh... and she's proud of you." Well, I made that one up, but he was a successful businessman with lots of money. I thought it couldn't hurt.

"She said that about me?" John asked in a way that made me think he wasn't talking about his business.

"Yes. Absolutely." I maybe said that too strongly.

John straightened up and wiped the tears off his face with the back of his blue button-down shirt. "We should go," John's tone was suddenly cold. A chill ran down my spine.

"But, don't you want to know more?" Kat asked.

If I could have kicked her in the shin without John noticing,

I would have. I guess I was so convincing that I had Kat fooled. But I don't think John was fooled.

He turned his back to us and started walking to the staircase. Kat shrugged at me and turned toward the staircase. I eyed the spot where the blood had pooled so many years ago, at least according to John. I felt guilty for making up this communication with his dead sister.

"I'm sorry," I whispered to the spot on the floor.

I started to follow Kat. John was probably down on the first floor by then. "At least you got us out of here," Kat whispered back to me. "You made it up, right?"

"Yeah," I whispered back, hoping the acoustics in the place didn't carry our hushed voices down to the first floor.

Guilt washed over me again, and it was all I felt until the cold grip took hold of my arm.

I stopped in my tracks; the cold grip didn't let go. And then the female voice behind me whispered, "He didn't do it."

I look at Amber. "I didn't know what she meant until you showed me that headline. Then I knew."

Jason pulls the paper toward him and looks down at that glaring headline. "There's got to be more of the story."

I look at the upside-down picture of John trying to hide his face with his handcuffed arms. But I can still see his strong chin and solid jaw. No doubt it's him.

"He was never convicted," Amber says. "I found other articles that said so. They said they didn't have enough evidence. But I think the case is still open."

"We've got to go back to the convent!" Kat yells out.

"We've got to go to the police," Amber sternly says. "That's all we have to do. For right now anyway. They may need you later, Matty."

"Me?!" My eyes shoot open wide. "Why me?" I try not to whine, but sheesh.

"Because you're the one who's talked with her," Jason says.

"Oh no. I don't want the police looking at me like I'm crazy." And it's not just the police, it's the kids at school, the parents, the colleges I apply for. It's not like Nebraska is a hotbed of paranormal, or anything but normal, understanding. I'm going to be bullied from now until I move out of this state. And I don't even want to think what will happen when my parents find out.

"We've got to tell the police exactly what happened. We can't just go to them and say we think the brother didn't do it," Amber says.

"We *can* just not go to the police at all," I answer. Then I think about it. "Maybe she didn't even say it to me. Maybe I just imagined it."

Amber doesn't say anything. She just looks at me like she wants to say, *Do you really believe that?*

"That's why we need to go back," Kat chimes in. "To make sure."

"Maybe we can do it as an anonymous tip," I say.

Amber pulls her phone out of her pocket and hands it to me.

I take it automatically and then look at her.

"Go on," she says like she's handing a nail to someone who just said they can easily swallow nails. Like she's daring me.

I stare at the phone in my hand and imagine myself calling the police. *Hello officer, I'd like to report a... well...*

"Maybe we should go back to the convent." I'm suddenly on Kat's side.

"Look, Matty," Amber's tone changes to motherly. I don't like where this is going. "The police work with us all the time."

"They do?" Kat asks.

"They work with the psychics we work with," Jason says.

"Like LuAnn?" I say. I forgot that she isn't real. Or isn't human.

Amber ignores me. "No, we work with psychics from across the country from time to time. And they do too."

"The police? Here? In Nebraska?"

Amber nods her head, but I kind of don't believe her even though I should. I think she can tell.

"Remember that girl who went missing in Papillion last year?" Jason chimes in. "The teenager? They called in a psychic from Michigan to help find her."

"The one who ran away from home?" Kat asks. "And they found her in Chicago?"

"Exactly," Amber says. "They found her because the psychic told them exactly where she was."

"But she was alive. John's sister has been dead for, like, twenty years."

"They work with psychics for dead people too," Amber grabs my shoulders. "All I'm saying is, they don't get freaked out by psychics."

I look at Kat who just kind of shrugs her shoulders.

"So what's it gonna help if they know John didn't do it? That's all I know."

"You could clear his name," Amber says.

Kat and I stare at her. I really don't think this will work, to just call the police out of the blue and tell them that a ghost told me John Abernath didn't kill his sister? That seems crazy to me.

"Maybe they're right," Jason says plainly.

"Oh no, not you too," Amber says.

"Think about it," Jason stands up and starts tossing a little foam ball in the air. "All we can tell the police is that we think John didn't do it based on Matty's shaky testimony."

"We have to go back there," Kat says. "We're so close to figuring out what she wants."

We all stare at Amber. She stands up, goes to her purse, and grabs the keys to the convent.

Amber stands in front of the convent doors. "We really shouldn't be doing this..." she says as she jiggles the keys.

"Wait!" I say before she inserts the key into the door. "Let's say a spell of protection." I grab Amber's hand, and then, hesitantly, Kat's hand. I hope my palms aren't sweaty. Kat grabs Jason's hand.

Amber asks for a wall of protection around us, and to keep us safe.

That makes me feel better that Amber, with her willingness to actually return to the convent, is not under the influence of LuAnn or anyone... *anything*... else.

Amber then opens the big doors and we step into the cement-walled, damp main entrance. This time the daylight is fading. We have flashlights in hand. Amber asks, "Where did you have your communication with Elsabeth?"

"Who?"

"The nun. She wasn't a nun, remember. Her name was Elsabeth."

"How do you know that's her name?" Kat asks.

"The newspaper article," Amber whispers. "It would probably help if we called her by her name rather than 'the nun.'"

"She talked to me right here, pretty much," I whisper back.

"And the first time you saw her—"

"The morgue," Kat says like we're walking through a haunted house at Halloween.

Jason whispers, "I would guess she probably doesn't spend a lot of time in the morgue."

"Agreed," I say. "I think she just wanted my attention."

"John said she was killed in the sanctuary," Kat recalls.

"But you didn't feel anything there?" Amber asks me.

I shake my head "no." Then I say, "But I don't feel anything here, either."

Amber motions for us to follow her into the sanctuary. The room is freezing cold, even though it's like, a hundred degrees outside. The room is colder than usual, in fact. Amber leads us to the center of the sanctuary. "Elsabeth?" Amber's voice echoes off the walls and seems to roll around the balconies that surround us.

Kat is behind me and holding onto my t-shirt so tightly the collar is stretched across my neck. She's so close I can feel her breath on the back of my neck. Have to admit, I kind of like it.

Jason hits the record button on the voice recorder he brought, just in case Elsabeth decides to talk and we can't hear her with our own ears. "Elsabeth? We'd like to talk to you. You remember Matty? She can see you. She'd like to talk with you."

Well, I think, *let's not go putting words in my mouth!* But I swallow my fear and manage to squeak out, "Elsabeth?" I clear my throat. "We know your story. Well, part of your story, but we'd like to know more."

Nothing.

"I don't think she's here," I say.

"Someone's here," Amber says.

"I think so too," Kat grabs my shirt even tighter.

"How do you know?" I ask.

"It's colder in here than it was when we were investigating," Amber says. "And it's eighty-six degrees out right now. Someone has to be here." She hands me an infrared thermometer, "See if there are any fluctuations in temperature. And Kat, get out the K2 meter and get a reading in the room to see if there is an electromagnetic charge."

"Where's the K2?" Kat asks.

"Back pocket of my backpack," Amber whispers.

Kat digs the K2 out and gets a reading. "The K2 is at a solid one-point-oh." Kat steps away from Amber and moves the meter slowly through the air, up and down. "One-point-oh," she says again.

"That's weird," Amber says. "What's the temperature, Matty?"

"Seventy-five."

"I guess that's why equipment helps sometimes. I could swear it was colder in here than it should be."

"Yeah, I thought it was colder too," Jason says.

"I told you," I say gently, "she's not here." I start to move toward the stairs to the balcony; Amber, Jason, and Kat follow me. With each step I take up the stairs, a feeling of dread fills my lungs. I don't know if *she's* here, but someone, or something is here.

"I don't like this," Kat whispers, her hand is again clutching the back of my shirt.

I ignore her and keep moving up the stairs. The last of the day's glowing sunlight is streaming in through a window at the landing. It seems weird to have a ghostly feeling when the sun is still out. I walk into the beams of light and cross over to the shadow side of the balcony. Kat, Jason, and Amber follow behind.

"You won't find her here." It's LuAnn. I haven't seen her since Amber told me about the spell of protection.

She starts to cackle in a way that sounds distant and echo-ey.

"Did you hear that?" I ask.

"Hear what?" Jason raises the voice recorder as if trying to get a signal.

"Nothing. It's not her. She's not here." I don't know why I trust LuAnn of all people—er—spirits.

"Where now?" Kat asks.

I wait to let LuAnn answer. I'll have to talk to Amber and Jason about this LuAnn thing later. In the meantime, I think through the spell of protection again. *Spirit guides, please surround me with a white light of protection...*

Suddenly the K2 Kat is holding beeps loudly and rapidly. "What the...?" Kat says as she looks at the display. Lights are flashing.

Amber grabs the K2 and shakes it, as if it's defective. It stops abruptly.

"What was wrong with it?" Kat asks.

Amber opens the back cover and spins the batteries around, then clicks the cover back on. "Don't know. Just a fluke."

She hands the K2 back to Kat and it again beeps wildly.

I hear LuAnn's crazy cackle and roll my eyes.

"Ignore it," I say pointedly.

Amber gives me a confused look over the flashing lights of the K2.

"It's LuAnn," I say, annoyed.

Amber drops her hand with the device to her side. "She's back?"

"I think she's trying to help us, but she's having some fun with us too."

Kat sidles up closer to me, if that's even possible. But I like it, and try not to at the same time.

"LuAnn," Amber steps away from us. "Can you take us to Elsabeth?"

"Such a weird name," Kat says.

"Weirder than LuAnn?" I say.

"Right," Kat responds.

"Girls," Amber says. "Focus. Matty, keep an ear out."

"LuAnn," Jason calls out, "please take us to Elsabeth."

Amber asks, "Can you help us?"

"What about your theory that LuAnn could be a demon or something?" I whisper. Again, I hear her cackle.

"I don't think she is," Amber says.

"Why?"

"I don't know. Just a feeling. What do you think, Jason?"

"I agree. She's a prankster, but she doesn't seem demonic. I mean, based on what Matty is telling us."

"So, who was the shapeshifter?" I ask.

"Hard to say," Amber whispers.

And now, the K2 abruptly stops beeping and there is a dead calm around us. We stand stock still and all I can hear is Kat's heavy breathing. I try not to be distracted by it.

"Room 210." Plain as day, I hear LuAnn's voice.

"Room 210," Amber and Jason whisper simultaneously.

"I heard that," Kat says.

I can't believe they heard it too. That means LuAnn isn't a figment of my imagination.

"This way." Amber points to a hallway that leads off the balcony. The one that seemed to give the former nuns direct access to the sanctuary.

15

Room 210 looks like any other room. It's bigger than a bedroom, like it was a holding room for the nuns or something before Sunday services. I suddenly get a funny image of them in here smoking, habits and all. I know it's not a true "image," just my twisted imagination. The room is sparkling clean, like the rest of this building. It's just an empty room, with glistening tiled floors and off-white walls. Wood trim makes it look fancier than most rooms. There are two average-sized windows facing out to another brick wall. I guess it's some twist in this weird building. No sun is coming in here. Maybe this was where they had Sunday school classes for neighborhood kids?

A blast of cold hits us like a wall of air-conditioned air.

"Do you feel that cold?" I ask.

"Freezing," Jason says.

Kat backs away and says, "I'm not going in there."

Amber turns to her and says something. I go ahead into the room. I am holding the infrared thermometer out in front of me. I watch the reading on the display drop. 60 degrees, 50 degrees, 40 degrees. It keeps dropping the further I get into the room.

Then the door slams shut behind me. The sound of it reverberates in the room. I swing around to the door. Amber,

Jason, and Kat are still in the hallway. But now Amber is pounding on the door. "Matty!"

I run over and turn the handle. Number one: it won't budge. Number two: it's ice cold and I can barely touch it. Just like last time, it burns my hand.

The thermometer is down to 32 degrees Fahrenheit. The point of freezing.

"Guys, the doorknob won't budge and it's freezing in here!" I try not to panic. A true ghost hunter doesn't panic. But I think I've been traumatized by the last time this happened: My heart is racing and if my brow could break into a sweat, it would, but it's just too cold.

"I can't get it to open either!" Amber yells.

"Let me try," Jason yells. I hear the doorknob jiggle and then I hear what sounds like kicks on the door. "It's solid wood!"

"Matty!" Kat sounds panicked.

"Stay calm!" I don't know if Amber is talking to me or to Kat.

I answer back anyway, "I'm trying." I dig a digital voice recorder out of my pocket and start recording.

"Say a spell of protection, Matty," Amber yells. "Right now!" The thumps on the door continue.

I start to call on my spirit guides to keep me safe and surround me with a protective light.

Just then I see movement out of the corner of my eye. A shadow darts into the corner and disappears.

I say the spell of protection again, more frantic.

And then, everything seems calm.

For a moment.

There's an ice-cold grip on my shoulder.

I turn around and see the shimmering image of Elsabeth. She moves like a sheet in the wind. Kind of fluttering and soft. She isn't solid like her ice-cold hand would have indicated. I can see through her, but still, she's pretty solid.

"Please don't show me your throat again. I know you were killed."

She takes a step away from me and smiles. It's a kind smile, as if she knows she has scared me but doesn't want to. Or maybe she pities me. I don't know. I feel so confused in this moment with her. As if someone else is taking over my thoughts, or trying to.

We stand there looking at one another for longer than any ghost hunter could expect to see an apparition.

"What do you want?" I say. "Can you speak?"

Her smile disappears and she shakes her head no. She grips her throat.

I throw my hand up in front of me and say "Got it!"

There's pounding on the door. "Matty?" Amber says, "Talk to me."

I turn my attention to the door briefly, then back to Elsabeth. It's like her signal is getting weaker. She's fading out fast.

I put the thermometer out in front of her. I want to invite her to take some of the battery charge if she needs it.

She places her hand over mine; the device between us.

Her signal is still weak but a little stronger.

She points to the corner where I saw the shadow.

"Matty!" Amber is more insistent now, but I feel like I have so little time left with Elsabeth. I try to ignore Amber.

"That shadow? That's the evil that killed you?"

I actually feel her fingers squeeze on top of my open hand. She nods her head.

"Your brother didn't kill you," I say.

Her face turns from sad to hopeful. She nods.

"Okay. So your brother didn't kill you. Who did?"

She points to the corner and I hear her otherworldly voice rasp out, "Help her."

"Help who?" I reluctantly look away from her to the empty corner of the room. "I don't see anything," I say. There's nothing. It's just a corner of the room.

When I look back at Elsabeth, she's gone. My infrared thermometer battery signal beeps once, then the device screen is completely blank. "Damn," I whisper.

There's still pounding on the door—hard, frantic.

"It's open," I yell. I don't know how I know, but I know. I guess because the room feels so vacant and calm.

I hear the knob turn and the door opens right up.

****

Kat gives me a big hug. "We were so worried."

I feel weird. Not because of Kat's hug but because of what just happened. I feel like there's a film of soot or something over me. Like I've been slimed or something.

"Are you okay?" Amber is calm. Her voice is soothing.

"Um... yeah? I guess."

Jason is inspecting the room and door. "What the hell happened in here?"

Kat holds my hand. It confuses me at first, but then I don't care. I only care about who did it. Like Elsabeth is still with me. Haunting me.

Maybe she is.

"She's gone," I say. I feel sad. Empty.

"What happened?" Amber says.

Kat looks around the room.

"I said she's gone!" I pull my hand away and kind of snap at Kat. I'm just so frustrated... for more than one reason.

"How can you be sure?" Kat makes a terrible investigator. She can't seem to tune into energies when she needs to.

"Kat, go stand over there. Back against the wall," Amber says.

It's almost like Kat has been sent to stand in the corner. "But not that corner!" I say quickly. "Anywhere but that corner!" I point to where I saw the shadow.

Kat stands awkwardly, mid-wall, with her back leaning against it. She slumps down to the floor and takes out her phone. I can't tell if she's pouting or relieved. Well, since when could I ever get a read on her?

Amber grabs my shoulders and looks me dead in the eyes. "What happened?"

I tell her and Jason everything... about the shadows in the corners and the nun who's not a nun who appeared and told me that her brother didn't kill her.

"Shit." That's all Amber says.

"Yeah. For sure." I agree. "So now what?"

Jason grabs the digital voice recorder from my hand. "You got it."

"Huh?" I look down at the recorder. "What do I have?"

"You hit the record button. Just like we taught you to do."

"Let's go back to the warehouse and plug this baby in!" Amber goes out into the hallway.

Kat is still playing on her phone.

I can't seem to move.

"Come on!" Amber says.

I look at Kat and we both follow Amber and Jason out into the hallway and outside the creepy convent.

The warehouse is completely dark when we get there. Like it's a ghost of a building. Amber turns on the lights and they flash on like fluorescents in a schoolroom.

She sets up the equipment that we need and sits down. "Give me the voice recorder."

I hand it over to her and reluctantly sit. All the way on the drive here I just kept thinking about it all. Who does Elsabeth want me to help if not her?

Amber has headphones on. She points to another set next to her. Lines flash up and down on the monitor in front of her, glowing ominously. I cautiously sit next to Amber and place the headphones over my ears. Kat and Jason stand behind us, staring at the monitor that is about to show the audio snake across the screen. Now I know why the lines are flashing all over the place.

I look at Amber and she looks a little pale.

I swallow hard. I don't know why I'm surprised. This is all exactly what I heard. An echoey voice of a young woman. Menacing groans in the distance. Growling.

"It wasn't my brother," she whispers, her voice gurgling as if the wound in her throat is still there, blood bubbling into her vocal chords. "Help Kelsey."

"Kelsey?" I ask.

"That's what I heard. Kelsey. Right?" Amber says. She stands up and tells Jason to listen. I stand and give my headphones over to Kat.

Jason nods when he gets to the spot. "That's awesome!"

"She said Kelsey, didn't she?" Amber asks.

"That's what I heard."

"Who's Kelsey?" Kat asks.

"I don't know," Amber looks to me.

I shrug. "Beats me."

"Um… did you hear the rest of this?" Jason pulls the headphone plug out of the computer and the sounds come through the speaker.

"Wow," Kat takes the earphones off.

"What, what?" I ask.

That's when I hear something unexpected. It's LuAnn. That crazy lady was there too. "Matty, run!" That's what I hear her say, then I hear her scream as a loud growl seems to overtake her voice.

I scootch back from the table. Jason stops the recording.

"Matty?" Amber is holding my shoulders.

"That was her. That was LuAnn."

Kat scootches back from the table now too.

"That scream?" Amber asks.

I nod my head.

"Are you sure?"

I feel like saying yes, with all certainty I'm sure. But maybe I misheard her. Maybe it wasn't LuAnn.

I take a deep breath. "Let's listen again."

Kat comes in closer and drapes her arm over the back of my chair. I hate that I like it.

Jason rewinds, and then plays.

Same thing. I hear LuAnn's voice yell, "Matty, run!" and then I hear her scream.

Jason looks to Amber with his finger hovering over the STOP button. Amber twirls her finger in the air as if to say "Let's keep going."

There's silence for awhile and then a scratching sound. Like a cat in a litter box, but, like, a really big cat. It sends chills up my spine. THAT, I did not hear.

Then I hear Elsabeth again. What she says makes the hair stand on the back of my neck. "No." But it isn't the word itself, it's the way she says it. More like a cry. "Nooooo." And it's almost as if I can see her being dragged by her hair as she's holding onto the man's hands, the same hands that are clutching her hair and dragging her—

I don't want to, but I close my eyes. I try to see the man, try to get a good look at his face. Then her voice calls out on the recorder, "Matty..." She says my name matter-of-factly, without emotion. Almost like she's resigned, but there's still a bit of hopefulness in her tone.

And then I see the man's face. And I know that I've seen it before.

Kat was right: The man was the ghost from my school. The one that touched me in Mrs. Piorzini's class. That's how he knew my name.

"We have to go back in there and help LuAnn."

"What?" Amber says.

"She was dragged into the dark by that... that shadow... that man."

"What man?!?" Amber grabs me by the shoulders and looks into my eyes.

Kat stands up and says, "From English Lit!" It's about as excited as I've heard her. "I saw him there too. I knew that's how he knew your name."

"LuAnn was screaming. We thought *she* might be the dark thing, but we were wrong—she was trying to help me. She *did* help me. And now she's in trouble."

"And Elsabeth too," Kat joins us in the middle of the room.

"Yes!" I agree.

"No!" Amber quickly and loudly responds.

We stare at her. "But..." I start to say.

"Look," Amber's eyes go from one to the other of us, but mostly, they land on me, "this is a different realm. We can't go 'in there.' There is no 'in' 'there,'" She uses air quotes to emphasize the two different words.

"What do you mean? I was 'there!'" I air quote back.

"You weren't," Amber shakes her head quickly. "Matty, you were nowhere near 'there.' And if it tries to drag you into 'there,' we are in big trouble, because I don't know how to get you out."

"But we have to try," I whine.

"From what you've described, I think LuAnn can take care of herself," Jason says, "Just wait. She'll be back."

"How can you be so sure?"

Kat is watching the conversation between the three of us and her head is bobbing back and forth. I wish she'd help me out here.

"She's a pretty strong spirit, wouldn't you agree? I mean, she can show herself to you, but no one else. How does she do that?"

Well, I thought it was me that did that, but okay—I did have to concede that LuAnn is a pretty strong spirit.

"And Elsabeth?" Kat asks. I don't know why she's so concerned about her all the sudden.

"Elsabeth has been through this before. What just happened to her may even be residual."

"But she yelled my name," I plead, "How can that be residual?"

"Maybe you were there..." Kat says.

I take a moment to have my mind blown.

I guess Amber feels the same, "She has a point. Maybe you were there."

"What?!?"

"Maybe you were one of the nuns."

16

The drive back to Fremont is quiet. I mean, I was quiet. Kat, not so much.

"Do you think you really could have been one of the nuns?" she asks. Well, really she just says it. She's just kind of talking without taking a breath. "That was so freaky. I just can't believe it. All we could hear was all this banging and you weren't saying a word. Amber kept trying to open the door…"

She keeps going, but I just keep replaying that moment in time when I was standing face-to-face with Elsabeth. Her brother didn't kill her. It was that man—the one I've seen in school.

The man gave me the creeps the first time I saw him and tonight I got an even better look at him. He's tall, like 6 feet or so, maybe more. And muscular. He has this scrappy beard and these piercing blue eyes. I remember his eyes so well—it's like they looked right through me. I guess he was kind of handsome in a creepy way. If you like that sort of thing, which I do not.

But why would he visit me at school? What did he want with me?

Kat continues on with her free-mind talking, "… I thought I was going to die when I heard that recording. Did you hear that when you were in the room?"

She finally takes a breath. The silence in the car is better than a playlist on my phone.

That's when I realize that I'd seen the man even before English Lit. I was in my Creative Writing class; now I remember because I thought then that maybe my imagination had gotten the best of me. Our assignment was to rewrite a famous line from somewhere and put it in a story, with a twist. I was writing about these gangsters when the man showed up.

I didn't think he was a gangster, but he wore a suit and a tie. I thought he was the dead grandpa of one of my classmates because he kind of looked like him.

The man was staring at me; that was what was so disconcerting. He wasn't looking at the classmate at all; just me. And then he disappeared.

"When did you know you were a lesbian?"

Another zinger from Kat.

"What?"

"Like, when did you know? Did you like a girl and then know? Or was it something like I've heard on tv, where you always knew."

"Ummm…"

"Nevermind," she says. She seems dejected.

"No, it's okay," I say. "I mean, I guess I always knew? I mean I didn't know because I didn't know what a lesbian was, but I knew I liked girls."

"Like, you were in love with them or something?"

"No. I mean, were you in love with boys when you were little?"

She snickers at that.

Silence.

She never did answer me.

Sleep doesn't come easy that night. Between my conversation with Kat about being gay and the screams of LuAnn that just won't leave my head, I keep tossing and turning. I'm also trying to figure out that guy, the one Elsabeth said murdered her. Why did he show up at school? What's his deal? More importantly, why is he watching me, following me? Will he show up here?

I put my pillow over my head and scream into it. When I release my grip, I feel a hand on my ankle.

I sit up in bed and see, at the foot of my bed, LuAnn. But she's not solid this time, like she's appeared to me before. She's fuzzy and fading in and out.

"LuAnn! Are you okay?"

"Matty." Her voice is like it's in a tunnel. No, more like a funnel. Like the big end is at her side of things but the little end is on my side of things and by the time her voice reaches my ears it cuts in and out. "Stay away."

"Stay away? From what?"

"The convent."

"Yeah, but..." I start to protest.

"Stay away."

And then she disappears.

I grab my phone and start to text Amber. "LuAnn just showed up." Send.

I think for a minute. Then I text, "We need to go back to the convent."

Send.

17

The next morning, I wait until Mom and Dad leave for work, and before Sasha wakes up so that no one has a chance to ask me where I'm going. I make the drive to Omaha by myself this time.

Jason's at work but Amber is able to meet me outside the convent. She asks what happened. We're standing in the shade of the tall entrance. Even though it's hot today, it's almost cold where we stand. Like sunlight never touches this spot.

"LuAnn showed up and told me we need to go back in," I lie.

"And do what, exactly?"

"I..." I have to think quick. And then I wonder what it is I think I'm going to do. "I... she wants us to..." The birds are chirping all around my lies.

"Look, we can't just go in there, unarmed, the two of us. Too much has happened. We have to get organized. Do another ghost hunt. Be intentional. Especially after what happened last time."

I look up at the big, heavy doors in front of us. "Yeah. You're right."

"I still don't trust LuAnn," Amber looks up at the doors with me.

"I didn't at first either, but then I saw her dragged away by that thing."

"What if she *is* that thing?"

"What do you mean?"

Amber grabs me and motions for me to sit down on the steps with her. "Matty, have you ever wondered if LuAnn *is* the darkness?"

"Not anymore," I say. "I think she's a guide for me."

"Really? Who brought you *here*?"

"Kat."

"Kat brought you to Jason, but who brought you here?"

"Well, I guess... LuAnn did?"

"And who brought you back the second time?"

"The nun... I mean John's sister... the nun in hiding."

"Didn't you tell me LuAnn told you to come back?"

"Maybe." I look at my Chucks. I don't even know what to think.

"And this time? Who brought us here?"

"LuAnn," I say softly. Crap, this lie is one I can't get out of.

"So if the darkness swallowed her up and took her off screaming, how did she communicate with you this time?"

"She somehow broke through the darkness?"

"I'm not so sure."

I kick a loose piece of cement with the toe of my shoe. I really want to go back in there.

"Look," Amber puts her arm around my shoulder, "let's get the team together. Let's do some more research. Let's get to the bottom of this... *without* LuAnn."

"But..." I feel my throat tighten, and I feel scared. "What if she comes back to me? What do I do?"

"Are you saying a protection spell?"

I don't know that I really need protection from her, and it's hard to believe, but I don't want her to go away. "But what if LuAnn has information for us?"

"She would have told you by now. She's playing with you and you need to protect yourself."

I want to tell Amber that *this* time LuAnn told me to stay away. This time, *I'm* the one who brought us here.

"You have my cell phone number. Call me. Day or night. Let me know what's going on. She can't get the best of you right now."

"Even in the middle of the night."

"Yep. Even then."

I suddenly wonder about Amber's life. Like, does she have a boyfriend? "Promise me, Matty."

"Okay. I promise."

"If LuAnn makes contact with you..." she leads me.

"...I call you right away."

"Day or night," she says.

"Day or night," I repeat.

Amber squeezes my shoulder and tells me to meet the team tonight at the warehouse.

Nunzi, Troy, Sara, Amber, and I are sitting around a table waiting for Kat and Jason to show up. Jason actually drove all the way to Fremont and back just to bring her here. He didn't want me driving back and forth to get her.

It was a long day in Omaha, but I basically went to the Old Market and walked around. I had a panicked moment when I thought I saw my mom at a place having lunch, but it wasn't her. Close call. I tried to text Kat a few times but she didn't answer. I texted Mom and told her that I was going to a movie with friends tonight, and then I went to a matinee. I knew Mom wouldn't be there and it killed some time.

When Kat and Jason walk in, I fight the urge to run over and throw my arms around Kat. I'm so glad to see her. But she doesn't seem very happy to see me. She's freezing me out or something. I guess she's mad that I came to Omaha and met with Amber without her?

"Hey," I say to her, hoping it will chip away the ice. Nothing. No response. "'Sup?" I act like I'm all cool, trying to get some kind of smile or reaction from her.

Nothing. Ice cold. *What's her deal?*

Everyone settles into chairs at a round table and starts strategizing about how to get rid of the darkness that sucked LuAnn away.

"The darkness isn't the problem," I hear the voice loud and clear in my right ear. It's LuAnn's voice. I look around the table but no one seems to hear her. And Kat just glares at me. I stand up and walk away from the table to hear LuAnn better.

"What LuAnn?" I whisper.

"The darkness isn't the problem. You're all focused on the darkness, but you shouldn't be." If I could describe her voice, I would, but it's like she was talking through the surface of shimmering water. It faded in and out and sounded muffled.

"Matty?" Amber calls out from across the room.

I suddenly realize I'm standing in front of a wall with my back to all of them. I must look crazy. Am I talking out loud to LuAnn? Can they hear her voice too?

Suddenly Amber is standing next to me. "What's going on?" she asks in a soft voice.

"It's LuAnn. She says we shouldn't be focusing on the darkness."

Amber lets out a long sigh. "Matty..."

"Tell her!" LuAnn's voice cuts through whatever Amber is saying.

"I did!"

"The nun knows what needs to be done."

Amber is still gently talking to me when I blurt out the words LuAnn just said.

Now everyone is gathered around me—Amber, Nunzi, Jason, Sara, and Troy. Even Kat. She can't keep her icy exterior for long when crap like this happens.

Amber turns me to face her. I say, "The darkness isn't the problem!" I get it now. We've been focusing on the darkness ever since it trapped me in that room and took LuAnn away. But that's not what took us there in the first place. It was the nun; I mean Elsabeth. "We need to help Elsabeth. That was what we went there for. The darkness is diverting our attention!"

"Holy..." says Troy.

Everyone stands around me silently.

"Ask her how we do that," says Amber.

I think it's kind of silly to just repeat what Amber asked, but I say it anyway. "LuAnn, how do we help the nun?"

I hear LuAnn laugh.

"She's laughing."

"Laughing?"

I raise my hand and shush Amber. "She's gone."

"I think she's playing with us," Amber says angrily.

"Maybe not..." says Jason. "I mean, she's kind of right. The darkness has diverted us away from what we went there to investigate the second time."

"I'm telling you guys," Amber is speaking forcefully. "I think she is the darkness."

"But if she were," I say, "why would she be trying to get rid of the nun?"

"Maybe LuAnn wants to keep us from getting rid of *her*."

Nunzi exhales air through his mouth in a half-whistle.

"Whether or not she's the darkness," says Jason, "we need help."

Everyone is silent for a minute. I fidget, uncomfortable with the silence.

Then Amber and Jason say it simultaneously. "Jengi."

Sara and Troy repeat it, "Jengi!"

Kat and I look at each other. "What's a Jengi?"

Nunzi says, "Yeah, what's Jengi?"

"Who," Jason says.

"I'll call her right now," Amber steps away with her cell phone in hand.

"Jengi is a psychic," Sara says. "She's pretty well-known in paranormal circles."

"Jenga?" Kat asks.

"No, Jengi," says Troy, who is untwisting a paperclip, as if calling a psychic up on the phone and asking her to get involved with our paranormal investigation is no big deal.

"Like the game," says Kat.

"The game with an i at the end," says Jason.

"Like a Jedi!" I blurt out, trying to play this game with Kat.

"No, the i is pronounced like the i at the end of Benji," Jason's starting to get annoyed.

"Jeddy?" Kat's smiling now and my heart melts a little.

"No! Jengi! Jengi! Jengi!!"

Clearly Kat knows how to push her cousin's buttons.

"Sounds like something that should be after a hashtag," I chime in. "Hashtag Jengi."

"I left her a voicemail," Amber interrupts.

"I'll follow up again tomorrow. See if she can come down and help us," Jason's demeanor changes when Amber is in the room. He's more chill now.

"Where does she live?" I ask.

"Minneapolis. And actually," Amber turns to me, "it would be good for you to sit down and talk with her. She can help you control the activity around you."

I think I'd like that.

The drive back to Fremont that evening is less difficult than I thought it would be. Kat had to ride with me; she had no choice. Why would Jason drive her all the way back when I was going anyway? She was much warmer by the time we were just outside Omaha, mostly because she had so many questions for me.

I asked her if she wanted to come over to my house and Google Jengi.

We get to my house at about 9:00 p.m. No one's home so I text mom quick and tell her I'm home and that Kat and I are hanging out. We go to my basement room and sit in front of the computer.

Jengi's website comes up and we see that she does psychic readings, paranormal investigations, and has worked with *the* actual Ghost Hunters. "Cool," says Kat.

I see a man hovering around in the corner of my room. "Do you think she can really help me?" The man takes a step closer. He opens his mouth as if he wants to say something. I've learned not to be freaked out, but I'm just waiting for the maggots to come crawling out of his mouth like some bad Halloween movie. I shut my eyes tight and hope he goes away.

"Ignore him," Kat says.

She actually sees him. Thank god. Sometimes I think I really am going crazy.

She clicks through the screens of Jengi's webpage. "She's got a lot of experience. I guess we'll find out soon."

I open my eyes and the man in the corner is gone. But I know he's still here somewhere, watching me.

It's Saturday night and the team is meeting at the heavy wooden doors at 11:00 p.m. I told my mom that I was staying over at Kat's house, again. I think she has some hopes that maybe we're doing girly things together—braiding hair, talking about boys, reading Seventeen magazine, or some weird crap like that. I feel like she still has that fantasy of me, being more girl-like. Maybe she thinks this queer thing is just a phase. If she only knew.

Kat and I sit in my car and stare at those big doors, waiting for the rest of the team to arrive. This time with Jengi. She evidently drove from Minneapolis that afternoon and was excited to meet me. At least that's what Amber told me in a text earlier in the day.

"Why do we have to do this in the middle of the night?"

"It's easier to communicate with spirits in the middle of the night," I say.

"I wonder why? I mean, I have communicated with them at different times of day."

"I don't know. It just is." Clearly, we both still have a lot to learn about ghost hunting.

The van drives up next to us with Jason at the wheel. Amber is in the passenger seat. I feel a sense of relief when I see her.

"Hey," I yell to Amber as she gets out of the van, "do you

guys have ghostbusters equipment in there to catch these shadow people?" I was only half-kidding, and mostly hoping. It would be great if they had some little box that sucked up these things like a vacuum cleaner.

"You guys been here long?" asks Jason.

"Sorry we're late," said Amber. "Kid problems."

Kid? I didn't know she had a kid.

"We've been here awhile," says Kat.

"Matty, this is Jengi. Jengi, Matty." Amber sways her hands between us like Vanna White on *Wheel of Fortune.*

Jengi is rad. She's tatted and has a nose piercing, eyebrow piercing, and a few piercings on her ears. She has a tattoo on the right side of her neck and I can see it under the glow of a light on the convent grounds: It's a quote from Edgar Allan Poe written in the wing of a raven. It says, *They who dream by day are cognizant of many things which escape those who dream only by night.*

"Matty," Jengi extends her hand to shake mine. She has a thick leather bracelet on her right wrist.

"Hi." I suddenly feel shy. And lost for words. She's beautiful. Shoulder-length auburn hair with a few strands of purple, piercing blue eyes, and a raspy, kind of sexy voice. But beyond that she's just so cool. Cooler than anyone I've ever seen in Omaha. She's wearing black sweatpants with a low waist and a low crotch that are tight from the knee to the ankle. Ankle-high black boots, a droopy but fitted black t-shirt, and a long hoodie jacket over that. She's just too rad for words.

She kind of gives a knowing laugh, then says, "So you're like me."

Hell no, I think, *I'm nothing like you. But I wanna be.*

"A psychic."

"Oh... I..."

"When did you realize you had the gift?"

Gift? All those months in therapy and the shrink never called it a gift.

"I think she's still in the process of realizing that," says Amber.

"You get visits?" Jengi asks.

"Visits?"

"I'm Kat," Kat appears from behind me like a ghost. I jump.

"Jesus, Kat!" I say.

Kat extends her hand out to Jengi. "We googled you. You're cool."

That's one thing I love about Kat. She tells it like it is.

Jengi just gives a little laugh. She turns to Amber, "So tell me more about your nun."

I feel like I blew a big opportunity. I could have talked to her about all that's been going on. I could have told her that my parents think I'm crazy and so I keep all the visits from ghosts to myself. I don't tell her about the grandma that gently squeezes my feet at night, or the creepy man that shows up at school sometimes, or LuAnn. And I want to tell her everything. I want her to know what I've seen and ask her how she can help me. But I blew it. And now we're moving on to the case at the convent.

"We can talk later," she says to me, as if she's read my mind, and she walks to the van with Amber.

I follow behind.

"What do you think?" Kat whispers to me.

"She's awesome!"

"Yeah, she's… awesome," Kat almost sounds disappointed.

This girl is going to be the death of me.

Once we all get organized, Amber takes me into the sanctuary with her and Jengi. Talk about disappointment: I've never seen Kat sulk before.

Amber is holding the K2 meter, I have a digital voice recorder, and Jengi is hands-free. She said she doesn't like the distraction of devices. She just needs to listen.

We're walking slowly and quietly. Jengi has her head held high, as if she's listening for anything in the balcony. We follow her.

The air feels like it's charged with static electricity and the K2 meter beeps every now and then to confirm that.

"She's here... somewhere," I whisper. I just don't know which who is here... LuAnn or Elsabeth. My guess is Elsabeth because LuAnn doesn't cause such a reaction—she's kind of stealth that way.

Jengi doesn't say a word. She just points up into the balcony where I saw Elsabeth once before.

"The stairs are back there," Amber whispers and points to a side door.

We follow Jengi to the stairs and she goes up cautiously. "Has she ever hurt anyone?"

Before we came into the building, Jengi asked us not to give her any information. She wanted to make her own discoveries.

"No," says Amber.

"Just scared the crap out of us," I add.

The K2 meter goes crazy when we walk onto the balcony. Its beeping is constant and seems urgent.

"I'm Jengi. Who are you?"

I don't think Jengi can see her.

But I can.

Elsabeth is standing at the edge of the balcony about five feet in front of us. She's looking out into the chapel as if she wants to be with us but doesn't at the same time. Jengi is looking right past her toward big open space.

"She's there," I point.

"You see her?" Jengi sounds surprised.

"Yes. Right there," I can't believe she can't see her. What kind of a psychic is she anyway?

Elsabeth turns toward us. She's facing Jengi. I step behind Jengi a little bit as Elsabeth again exposes that gaping wound where there is a mess of blood red tissue and what I think is her windpipe.

I close my eyes tight and fight the urge to run with everything I have in me.

"Who did that to you?" Jengi asks.

Well, she must see her now because we never told her anything about this.

All I hear is an eerie rasping. And a throaty gurgling. I make sure the digital recorder is going.

"It wasn't her brother," Jengi says to Amber. "She knows you have concerns about that."

"You can make out what she's saying?" I can't believe it.

Jengi holds her hand up as if to tell me to stop talking. "She wants us to go to the crypt."

Chills run down my spine.

Amber squeezes my shoulder. I know I have to do it. I have to go back down there. I take a deep breath.

"Be careful." I hear LuAnn's voice loud and clear. I look at Jengi to gauge her reaction.

"That was your spirit guide," Jengi says matter-of-factly.

"That was LuAnn!" I'm not really surprised that LuAnn is my spirit guide. I'm surprised that Jengi figured it out from the first moment.

"You heard her?" Amber asks Jengi.

"Yes. And Matty, that's your spirit guide."

"Oh great," I half-laugh. "LuAnn is kind of mean."

"She's a trickster for sure," says Jengi, "but she's not mean. She's trying to help you."

"She's been trying to keep me away; at least until she got swept up by the shadow."

Jengi is silent for a moment, then says, "She kept the shadow from sweeping you away, but she's fine."

I can't believe what I'm hearing. That crazy old lady helped me?

"She helps you with the other spirits too. She's glad you're working with Amber."

Sure. Now LuAnn's an open book. Why didn't she just tell me all this stuff?

"Shall we?" Jengi opens her hand toward the door.

Like she wants me to lead! Uh-uh. No way. "After you," I say.

"Smart girl," I hear from the air. Maybe LuAnn is watching out for me.

Amber decided that we needed to reorganize the group before we went down to the crypt, so we're back at the van. Nunzi and Sara are going to sit in the sanctuary in case there's any activity there again. Amber tells Kat to stay in the van with Jason and Troy to monitor the few cameras that have been set up. Kat actually looks relieved. It's perfect for her; she doesn't have to admit how terrified she is about going in, and she gets to be part of the investigation anyway. Her cool factor is still in check.

Mine, however, is non-existent. I'm going in with Amber and Jengi. "And what are we going to do once we get in there?"

"Well," Amber says, "that's where your role is super important."

I take a deep breath.

Amber grabs hold of my shoulders. "Look at me."

I look her directly in the eyes.

"You need to stay strong. For some reason, this spirit, and the spirits here are drawn to you. Take this." Amber puts a stone in my hand and closes my fingers over it. "It's Black Tourmaline. It would be better if it was charged with your energy, but some kind of protection is better than none."

"We'll be with you every step of the way," Jengi says.

Okay. Wait a minute here. They're making it sound like

I'm going to be in charge or something. Or a beacon. Or they're going to make me walk in first while they cower behind me like the Scarecrow and Lion following Dorothy into the haunted forest. Maybe some flying monkeys will be swooping down on us.

I gulp down my fear. "What am I supposed to do once I'm in there?"

"I'll be doing most of the work," says Jengi.

I can feel the tension leave my shoulders right away.

"I'll try to make contact with the nun."

"Her name is Elsabeth," I chime in.

Jengi seems to ignore me, "It's clear that she wants to tell us something. She said she won't leave here until we help her."

"She definitely has unfinished business," says Amber.

"Ya think?" comes out of my mouth without thinking. "Sorry."

Jengi and Amber ignore my sarcasm. Thankfully.

"You may need to talk to her too," says Jengi.

"And say what?"

"Ask her if she'd like to tell us something. Ask her who murdered her."

Um, gee, that seems like a big question. "What about the dark shadow? It doesn't seem to want us there."

"I'll be working with the dark shadow while you and Jengi work with Elsabeth." Amber is always so fearless. I want to be like her someday.

"Shall we get ready?" asks Jengi.

I suddenly have visions of us getting into work overalls like the Ghostbuster women. But no, we gather our K2 meters, flashlights, digital voice recorders, and a thermal imaging camera. All I'm carrying is a digital voice recorder. I guess they figure that's enough for me to worry about.

When we face the big double doors I think about how many times I've already been here. I know exactly how to get to the crypt. I know exactly how to get to the room I was trapped in. I know exactly how to get to the balcony in the chapel. What I don't know is how to get out of going in yet again.

We walk down the long ramp that leads to the wide double doors of the crypt. When we open the doors we see the oven-like cutouts ahead of us in the stone wall. It's definitely cold enough down here to store dead bodies, and I'm sure that it's even colder in those oven-like cutouts where the bodies were placed. What surprises me most is that there are twelve cutouts in the wall. I counted them the first time I was down here. I mean, how many nuns died at a time? Did they store them down here until the ground thawed? Weird.

"Okay," Amber holds a device in the air. "I have level EMF readings right now."

"Turning on the digital recorder," says Jengi.

They both aim their flashlights at me.

"Oh yeah, turning on my digital recorder."

"Why don't you start," Jengi aims her flashlight at me again.

"Me?"

"Yeah, they seem to respond to you."

"Okay..." I thought Jengi was leading this thing? "Uh, is there anyone here with us?" I scan the room with my flashlight, like someone will pop out of a corner at any minute.

I feel a tap on my shoulder. "Was that one of you?"

"What?" Amber aims her flashlight beam at me.

"Someone just tapped my shoulder."

They both say no and then Amber examines my back and shoulders in the flashlight beam, waving the K2 around me. "The EMF is spiking."

Great. Just great.

"Who's here with us?" asks Jengi.

"Yeah, uh, who's here with us?" I really have to get this ghost hunting thing down. I just need to commit. "Is that you Elsabeth?"

Something slams to the ground in a corner of the room. All our flashlight beams wave around the room like we're in a dance club. As we're scanning corners and crypts and doors, I feel a strong squeeze on my shoulder. I turn around and there's Elsabeth.

I gasp her name. The flashlight beams behind me stop moving and Amber and Jengi are completely quiet until Jengi says, "Ask her what she needs from us."

I feel like a parrot. "What do you need from us?"

Elsabeth softly smiles, like she's happy we can see her.

She points to a crypt.

Our flashlight beams land on the crypt at the far right bottom corner of the room. "Go look," Jengi says to me.

You go look! I think. But I want to be a ghost hunter. A real ghost hunter. So, I guess I need to do this.

I go to the hole in the wall that Elsabeth pointed to and shine my flashlight. I fully expect to see bones but instead there's a necklace. I pull out the long, beaded strand. It has a cross hanging from it.

"That's a rosary," says Jengi.

I stand stock still with the rosary dangling from my hand. "Someone just tapped on my shoulder," I whisper loudly.

"It's another nun," says Jengi.

"You see her?"

"I see a heat signature on the thermal imaging camera," Amber says.

"I don't see her," Jengi says, "but I sense her standing behind you. She's gone now."

Elsabeth appears in front of me again.

"Ask her what the significance of the rosary is."

I sigh. This seems a bit silly. Why doesn't Jengi just ask herself?

"What's the significance of the rosary?"

Then Elsabeth does something I've never heard or read of before. She kind of melts down into the stone floor, and then rises up again like a mist.

I slowly step back to Amber and Jengi. That was just too freaky.

"Have you ever seen that before?" I ask the two of them as Elsabeth slowly fades away.

"Never," says Jengi.

Then my flashlight beam goes out and Amber's starts to flicker.

"She's trying to gain energy from us," Jengi says.

The room becomes ice cold.

"She's not done yet. There's something she needs to say."

"What's going on?" I ask. I'm starting to shiver but I don't know if it's from the cold in the room or from fear.

"She must have exhausted herself and now she needs to get energy from the room and from us to tell us what she wants."

"The thermal imaging camera battery just went dead," Amber says.

"What would you like to tell us, Elsabeth?" Jengi holds her voice recorder in the air. "If you talk into this microphone, we'll be able to hear you. You don't have to manifest again."

Just then I get a surge of energy rush through my body, like I just stuck my finger in a light socket, but not as jolting. And then I feel something in my body, like I can hear her but not her voice, just an impression of her.

The room is quiet. "The temperature is rising," Amber says. Our flashlights stop flickering.

"She's gone," Jengi says.

We stand stock still for a few minutes, but there's nothing in the room anymore.

We go back to the van and listen to the voice recorders. About halfway through my recording, just before Elsabeth turned into mist, we hear the name Kelsey. We listen back to the recording about a dozen times, each one of us taking a turn at the headphones.

"Clear as day," Jengi says. "Kelsey."

"Kelsey… just like Elsabeth said when I got trapped in the room, remember? But who's Kelsey?" I ask.

Amber says, "Good question."

"I need to go back in," says Jengi.

I'm hesitant, but Amber immediately says, "Let's go."

We put new batteries in our digital voice recorders and our flashlights.

It's a familiar sight by now, the big double doors leading into the small sanctuary where the confessionals are. I'm almost not afraid of it anymore.

When we stand in the small outer sanctuary our K2s go crazy. The electromagnetic field must be off the charts.

"It started here," Jengi says.

"What did?" I whisper back.

"That's all I'm getting. That it started here."

"Who's with us?" Amber asks as she sways her digital recorder in the air. "Kelsey? Elsabeth? Are you here with us?"

Then I blurt out, "LuAnn? Are you here?" and the K2 needles hit the top range of the meter. Their alarms sound out like dogs barking at a passerby.

"She wants us to say a prayer of protection," Jengi says.

It feels good that someone else can sense LuAnn. And has figured her out so easily. Before we go any further, we say, "Spirit guides, please surround us with a circle of protection. Keep us from any harm or danger and watch over us as we move into this space."

I always feel goofy when I say this stuff, but it does help, and I guess I'm getting more comfortable with it. I think I'd just feel better saying it in my head than out loud.

The K2s quiet down after we say it. Amber listens to the digital recorder and there's nothing, even after she asks for Kelsey and Elsabeth.

We move into the large sanctuary and we immediately hear a loud sound on the floor to the right of the altar. All our flashlight beams go to the exact same place at the exact same time.

"What was that?" asks Amber.

"Sounded like a 100-pound bag of flour hit the floor," I say.

Jengi yells, "There!"

I follow her flashlight beam up to the railing of the balcony. I don't see anything.

"There was a shadow. It moved past the rail from right to left."

We're all silent as we listen and watch.

"Kelsey, are you here?" Amber's question slices through the silence.

Whap! The sound like a bag of flour hitting the floor comes from the same place as before.

"There!" Jengi says. "The shadow again!"

"Something's playing out," says Amber.

"Like a video?" I ask.

"Could be residual," Amber says.

"Start the voice recorders," Jengi says. "Let's ask some questions."

Amber and I both start recording, then Amber asks, "Who's here with us?" There's a pause.

"Do you have something you want to tell us?" I feel proud of myself for just blurting that out into the darkness. Pause.

"Can you tell us why you're here?" asks Jengi.

"Did you just hear that?" I ask.

"What?" whispers Amber.

"I heard a whisper. Just behind us."

"Let's listen to the audio," Amber says.

I guess they hadn't heard it. I couldn't make out what it said.

When Amber plays back the audio, we hear clicking sounds first, then, sure enough, we hear a whisper say, "Release." We have to listen to it two or three times to really understand what's being said, but it's clear as day once we get it.

"That's not Elsabeth," I say. It's weird that I know her voice by now.

"No," Amber agrees, "It sounds like a young girl."

"Start the recorder again," Jengi says. Amber turns it on and Jengi continues talking to the air. "We know it's hard to talk, but what would you like to say? We can hear you in this recorder."

"Release," Amber says to Jengi. "Do you think she wants to be released from here?"

"Yeah, whoever she is, she doesn't want to be here anymore," I say. I don't know where that's coming from, but it just feels right. "She never belonged here. She just came in one day."

"Because she heard screaming," Jengi says.

"You guys can hear her?" Amber points the digital recorder our direction.

"I can sense her more than hear her. I don't know; it's like the words are just coming into my head." This is such a weird feeling.

"Exactly," says Jengi. "That's exactly what it's like. It's an impression."

"Where would you like to go?" asks Amber.

"Kelsey, can you tell us what happened?" I just know this is Kelsey. I don't know how, but I do.

Then we just keep asking questions.

"Did someone get killed here?"

"Do you see any light? Can you go to the light?"

"Are you trapped here?"

"Do you want to go home?"

We pause after each question to make sure she has time to answer.

"Let's listen," says Amber. She hits the playback button.

"Where would you like to go?" the question plays back and we hear another whisper. Amber rewinds so we can listen, again and again and again, but we can't make out what's being said.

"Kelsey, can you tell us what happened?"

"Yes," is whispered.

We all look at each other during the pause and repeat "yes" to each other.

"Did someone get killed here?"

A scratchy voice says, "Yes. Saw it."

"Do you see any light? Go to the light."

"No. Dark."

"Are you trapped here?"

"Yeeesssss."

"Oh my god," I say.

"Do you want to go home?"

"Mama."

I take in a deep breath.

"I've never heard so many questions answered before," says Amber. "That was a legit conversation."

"Did you ever see anything about a young girl being murdered here during your research of this place?" asks Jengi.

"No. It's weird, isn't it?" says Amber.

"No one knows she's here," I say. And then I see her, clear as day. This is the girl I saw behind my tv set at home, and outside the library at school. But how could she be somewhere else when she's trapped here?

"Spirits don't know walls," Jengi says. I swear she must be able to hear my thoughts.

"She disappeared," I say.

"She's gone?" asks Amber.

"No, she disappeared from her life. She went missing."

"Yeah, I get that too," says Jengi. "We need to find out if there were any missing children around the time of the murder."

"Now she's gone," I say. "That was intense."

"Let's go outside for a minute," says Jengi. "Get some fresh air."

As we reconvene by the van, Jengi says to me, "It's important to take a break after something intense like that happens. You don't want them to drain everything out of you."

She was right. I did feel kind of drained.

Kat jumps out of the back of the van. "You did an awesome job. That was rad." She bumps her shoulder into my shoulder.

"Yeah… thanks," I say. I feel kind of weird.

"We caught something," Jason says.

Amber hops up into the van and motions for me and Jengi to climb in with her. It's close quarters but we manage to gather around the screen. Kat squeezes in behind me and I try not to think about her breath on my neck, in my ear.

Sara, Troy, and Nunzi stand at the back of the van, waiting their turn to come in and see the screens.

Jason is sitting in front of the monitor and freezes it on one frame in particular. "There," he points.

I can make out the outline of the girl's head, and I can see her face like she's looking out at us through a sheer curtain.

"That's her," I say, and Jengi agrees.

"Wow!" Amber says with the most surprise and enthusiasm I've heard from her yet.

"1976," Jengi says.

"What?" asks Amber.

"1976 is somehow significant."

"According to that article, that's when Elsabeth was killed," Amber says. She jumps out of the van and starts typing into her phone with her thumbs. I think at first she's texting someone but then she tells us she's doing a search for "missing children in Omaha 1976."

The rest of the team starts a search on their phones too.

"I wonder how Elsabeth and Kelsey are connected?" I ask.

"Maybe they aren't," Jengi answers. "Maybe Kelsey just wandered here and got stuck because she didn't know where she was."

"Can that happen?"

"Maybe she was attached to an object that someone brought here."

"Guys..." Amber sounds stunned. "I found something."

20

We huddle around Amber's small screen and see what she's staring at: *Twelve Year-Old Missing After Family Day at Memorial Park.*

"Memorial Park is right around the corner," Amber says as she scrolls down the screen.

"The girl's name was Susannah Kelsey."

"Whoaaaaa," Troy exclaims.

"So Kelsey is her last name, not her first," I say, obviously. Then I feel a strong pull. "I want to go back in."

"I think we've done enough tonight," Amber says.

"No," I'm more forceful than I intended. "We *have* to."

I guess my tone of voice is convincing because before I know it, we're back in the sanctuary.

"We have to go up there." I motion to the balcony.

"I feel like I need to stay down here," Jengi says. She's standing right on the spot where I sensed Kelsey, I mean, Susannah.

Amber goes up to the balcony with me and I look down at Jengi. We kind of nod at each other like we know we're exactly where each one of us needs to be.

Amber starts the recorder and everything is quiet for awhile.

I feel a cold sensation on my arms and warmth inside my chest. The hair on my arms stands up.

"What's going on?" Amber asks as if she knows something is happening but doesn't know what.

"She's here," I whisper and my whisper rises to the ceiling of the sanctuary.

"Are you Susannah Kelsey?" Jengi's voice floats up from the floor.

"Do you want to talk to us?" Amber asks.

"She's Susannah," I said, "I can feel her being excited that someone finally understands her."

"Are you stuck here?" Amber asks.

"Yes, she is." Amber doesn't need a recorder; I can hear Susannah's responses. "She wants to go home."

"Susannah, honey, home is different now. You need to find a light. Can you see a light anywhere?"

"A man is grabbing her. He's hurting her. She wants to go home. She keeps crying that she didn't see anything, but he won't let go."

"Can you see this?" Amber whispers.

"She's fighting him. Kicking and screaming. He's putting his hand over her mouth and she bites him. His hand tastes like tobacco. He's hitting her across the face. She's crying..."

I don't want to see this anymore but it plays like a movie and I can't make it stop.

"He's grabbing her throat and pushing her back against the rail. He's bruising her back and she can't breathe, can't cry, can't do anything. She's running out of air, she's passing out, she doesn't see anything but she can feel her body being lifted up and then she's tossed like a rag doll."

"Matty, Matty!" Amber is shaking me. I'm gasping for air.

"Elsabeth is here," Jengi says from below. "She wants me to follow her."

I'm still gasping when Amber asks if I'm okay. I just nod because my throat feels hot.

Amber grabs my hand and pulls me with her as she goes downstairs to meet Jengi.

"There. She wants us to go back to the crypt."

"Not again," I manage to say, although my voice is raspy.

"It's okay," Amber says trying to comfort me.

I'm not comforted.

But off we go to the crypt again. Jengi opens the heavy door and that cold whoosh of air hits us like it does every time. And as we walk down the ramp into the crypt the air gets colder and colder.

"Susannah left us when we walked down here. She doesn't like it here."

"But Elsabeth is here," Jengi says.

"There," Amber has put down the digital recorder and now she's using the thermal imaging camera. "I see a heat signature."

"Yes," Jengi confirms the location. "She wants us to look there."

"It's blocked out," Amber says.

Since I'm not looking, I don't know where "there" is.

I finally get the courage to look and see a crypt hole that's not a hole anymore. There are bricks lined up where the hole used to be. There are fourteen holes; not twelve like I originally counted. But two of them are bricked over. How did I not notice that?

Amber is pushing on the bricks. "They're cemented in."

Jengi's hands are now on the bricks as if she's feeling some kind of vibration in them.

"She can't rest until Susannah rests," I don't know where that came from, but I know that it came out of my mouth.

"What?" Amber turns her flashlight toward me.

"I...I don't know how I know. It's like, she told me, I guess. But... she said she can't rest until Susannah rests. It's her fault she died."

"It's not your fault," Jengi speaks directly toward where I see Elsabeth. "You didn't ask to be murdered. You didn't bring Susannah into the building."

"She's crying." I don't see her crying but I *feel* her crying. This is weird.

"Do you think Susannah is behind here?" Amber points to the brick. "I mean, her remains?"

"She's nodding," I say.

At the exact same time Jengi says, "Yes. She's in this one," she points to the lower blocked-out crypt. "The top one was blocked out to make it less obvious. It's empty."

"And Elsabeth," I step onto a stone on the floor, which is

made up of large stones in a random kind of pattern. The spot where Elsabeth liquified and came back as a mist.

"She's buried here," Jengi finishes for me.

"Well, we've got to get somebody in here to excavate," Amber says.

"The dark shadow," I cry out. I see it behind Elsabeth, creeping up out of the floor like dark smoke from a fire. I can't say anymore, I can only stand and watch as it overcomes Elsabeth and she's sucked away into the darkness.

Next thing I know Amber is shaking my shoulders and yelling my name.

I look at her but my eyes won't blink. It's like when you're tired and your eyes fix on one point and you don't want to blink—you just want to stare off into the nothingness.

"10-9-8-7," Jengi is looking into my eyes as she counts down. I don't know why, but it's helping me. I blink. "6-5-4-3-2..." I feel like I can breathe even though I didn't know I couldn't before. "One." She snaps her fingers as if to put an exclamation point on her countdown.

"There was darkness..." I say.

"I know. I saw it too," Jengi's voice is soft, motherly. "Don't let it take you too. When you see something like that, you have to stay with yourself. You have to stay outside of it."

"But, I wanted to help her...."

"I know, I know."

"What happened?" Amber asks.

"A shadow figure took over Elsabeth and pulled her back into the darkness," Jengi says, then turns to me. "She'll be okay; she's come back from this before, right?"

"What if..." I can barely get my question out. "What if releasing Susannah means unleashing the shadows?"

"You mean, angering them?" Amber asks.

"Yeah. Like, what if they go crazy?"

"Let's get Susannah released and safe first. Then we'll try to release Elsabeth. Once we know they're both be safe, we can deal with the shadow people."

"How?" I ask.

"Cleansing," both Amber and Jengi say at the same time.

It takes about a week for Amber to get things arranged for the excavation.

First, she had to call John Abernath. She said he cried when she told him what had happened. And he was more than happy to arrange an excavation. He hired some guys that had done work for him in the past.

Amber arranged for Jengi to meet us at the convent on a Monday. Jengi wanted to be there so she again drove down from Minneapolis.

I know I should have invited Kat to be here too, but, I don't know, things are kind of weird between us.

We talked on the phone a few days ago. When we talked, she was going on and on about some skateboarder guy she met at the skateboard park. He had a few tats and she found that uber-rad. I thought he must be out of high school if he has tats. Anyway, she made a point of her heterosexuality and it made me feel weird. I wanted to say, "Okay, okay, I get the point, you're into guys and not into me. It's fine. Let's move on." But I didn't. I just listened and made small agreement sounds throughout the conversation.

It sucks to be gay in a small town.

And anyway, this is where my life is at right now, standing here with Amber and Jengi while these guys chisel away at the concrete between bricks. John had intended to be with us here today, but he said it was just too painful and to let him know what we found.

I guess I kind of get it. I mean, I wouldn't want to see the skeleton of someone I loved either.

"Do you feel anything?" Amber's question doesn't seem to be directed to anyone in particular.

Jengi and I both say no. But I do feel something. I feel sorrow and relief all at the same time. I just didn't say anything because I don't know if it's coming from within me, or from somewhere else.

When I was in my last high school, in Denver, I kept seeing this little girl. She would stand by my bed at night and pull on my sheets. And during the day she would show up in my classes and roll my pencil around my desk. It got so I would just put the pencil behind my ear, but then it kept falling to the ground. Like the little girl was pushing it out from behind my ear. I even got in trouble in class once about it.

So then I kept it between my teeth. I could feel a pull on it and I'd chomp down harder. Then, one time, the metal from the pencil bit into my lip from the force of the pencil being pulled out and I yelped. Right there. In class. Everyone laughed... but not the teacher. She thought I had been throwing the pencil to the ground just to distract everyone, or get laughs, or something. So she sent me off to the principal's office.

I didn't tell her what was going on, but when my parents sat me down at the dinner table and pressed me for information, I spilled the beans.

Next step—psychiatrist. I had to go once a week forever, it seemed. She had me go through all sorts of tests—an MRI, a brain scan, neurological testing—I hated it. They didn't find anything, of course, so finally, she came up with the poltergeist theory and told my parents I needed to go on some meds.

My mom didn't like that. She stopped sending me to her, but the little girl didn't stop playing around with me.

If that doctor could only see me now. Standing in front of a crypt in an abandoned nunnery or whatever they call these things, with a ghost hunter and a psychic. #LifeIsWeird

These guys John sent chisel away at the concrete. Each strike of the hammer on the chisel makes me cringe. Like a dentist is taking a pickaxe to my teeth or something.

"Please be careful!" I yell. The men stop and look at me. It's just what I heard in my head. Something is in the crypt. I mean, *someone* is in there. I know it.

"Let's go upstairs and get a cola," Amber says and tries to gently move me away from the scene of the crime.

"No!" I pull away from her. "They want me to be here."

We watch as the men silently work. Chipping away, chipping away, chipping away. It seems like it takes forever before even one brick comes loose. They pull it away. One of them turns on a big flashlight and peers beyond the brick. He hands it to Amber and asks her if she wants to take a look.

Amber looks at me and Jengi. Moment of truth. We can all feel it.

She steps up to the bricked-over crypt. Shines the flashlight in the small hole left by the loose brick. Hands the flashlight back to the man and steps back to us.

"There are bones."

I let out a breath that I didn't even know I was holding.

"We need to call the police."

The men stop working and we all go back out to the van. Amber's hands seem to be shaking when she calls 911. Although this doesn't seem like an emergency to me. Not any more at least.

The remains in the crypt are Susannah Kelsey, the girl who had disappeared in 1976. And sure enough, they lifted the stone from the floor and found another skeleton there. That one was confirmed to be Elsabeth Abernath.

The police don't know who killed them. They think that Susannah had wandered into the convent the day Elsabeth was killed. Based on what we told them, they said that she must've seen Elsabeth's murder and the person responsible then killed Susannah. All I know is that whoever it is lives in the shadows.

"It's not our job to find out who murdered anyone," Amber says, "It's our job to help lost souls move on, and that's what we did."

Jengi took me back to the convent and we did a cleansing.

We lit sage and walked around and told the spirits to leave this place; that Elsabeth and Susannah had moved on and there was nothing here to hold onto anymore.

"But where do the shadows go?" I asked Jengi.

She didn't seem to have an answer for that, and I hope I never find out.

22

Elsabeth visits me in my dream again. This time she's holding someone's hand. I can't quite make it out. Then I realize it's her. The girl. They don't say anything, but I can tell they are at peace.

After they walk away, I turn around and realize that I'm in a house somewhere I've never been before. *There are more truths to discover.* These words come from inside me, or outside of me, I don't know which.

Go upstairs.

I hold onto an iron railing. There are ornate circles in the metalwork. I climb the stairs that curve up and into a hallway. Curtains flutter at the windows.

There are more truths to discover. It's not from inside of me, that voice. I know that now. I recognize it though.

There isn't any furniture in this house but people are moving back and forth. They're busy but they don't see me, or at least don't look at me. They just keep moving across the hall from room to room.

And then I hear a scream.

And then I wake up.

*****

The next day I'm picking Kat up to go have a cup of coffee. As she walks to the car I can tell she's brooding and I know I'm in for it.

"Hey," I say, trying to act cool but my voice sounds apologetic and scared.

"Jason told me about your adventure." She doesn't even look at me.

"Yeah?" Maybe if I act like I didn't do anything wrong. Like I had every right to go on the excavation without her. "It was all right." I'm not going to play up how amazing the whole thing was.

I start driving toward downtown Fremont to the one coffeeshop in town, which is exactly one mile from Kat's house. It's the longest mile I've ever driven. Kat is completely silent.

"We found them," I try to slice through the silence. "So, Elsabeth is in the light or wherever the spirits go when they…" Um… what the heck am I saying, "…go."

"Why didn't you call me?"

I pull up in front of the coffeeshop and put the car in park. "Well, it just kind of happened, I guess."

Kat stares at me for a minute as if she's trying to decide what to say.

And then it happens. Before I can even say "stop" or "go" or "hell, yes." Before I can even think about what's happening.

Kat puts her hand around the back of my neck and pulls me toward her. And she plants a kiss on my lips. A nice kiss.

"That'll teach you for leaving me out of things."

And then she opens the car door and gets out. And leaves me there wondering if she's playing a game, or if she's open to the possibility.

My phone starts buzzing in my back pocket. I fumble for it and it feels cool against my warm, flushed face.

"Hey Matty, it's Amber."

"Oh, yeah. Hi," I'm watching Kat walk to the door of the coffeeshop. Damn, she looks good. I feel myself opening up to her again, but I don't know if I should.

"Do you want to go to Savannah, Georgia?"

"What?"

"We're going to investigate a house in the Historic District. We could use you if you're open to it."

And that's the moment my life changed.

And there was no turning back.

Acknowledgments

This book couldn't have been written without the love and support of Marian Martin-Moran, Shannon Malloy, Kally Casper, and Hayley Frazee.

I'd also like to thank Amy Bruni and Adam Berry from *Kindred Spirits*. Because of their *Strange Escapes* trips, I was able to truly experience ghost hunting in various locations. I'm also grateful to Dana and Greg Newkirk from *Hellier* and the Traveling Museum of the Paranormal. And finally, Sarah Soderlund (aka Paranormal Sarah), whose psychic abilities absolutely amaze me. All these paranormal investigators inspired me in so many ways.

About the Author

Patti Frazee is the author of two adult novels, *Cirkus* and *Out of Harmony*. She has a BFA in theatre and an MFA in Creative Writing. A lifelong paranormal enthusiast, Patti has only recently been on actual ghost hunts. She lives in Minneapolis and has 14 nieces and nephews.

www.pattifrazee.com

Twitter: @pfrazee_author

Facebook: @PattiFrazeeAuthor

Instagram: pattifrazee1